XX v XY

THE FINAL WORLD WAR

A NOVEL BY CHRISTINA CIGALA
STORY BY BOBBY GOLDSTEIN

Post Hill
PRESS

A POST HILL PRESS BOOK
ISBN: 978-1-68261-409-9
ISBN (eBook): 978-1-68261-410-5

XX v. XY:
The Final World War
© 2017 by Christina Cigala
All Rights Reserved

Cover Illustration by Ashley Cole Bruce

Post Hill Press
New York • Nashville
posthillpress.com

Published in the United States of America

For all the weird girls.

I'm nobody! Who are you?
Are you nobody, too?
Then there's a pair of us—don't tell!
They'd banish us—you know!

How dreary to be somebody!
How public, like a frog
To tell one's name the livelong day
To an admiring bog!

–Emily Dickinson

PROLOGUE

I AM VERY UGLY. I know this because my beloved told me so. It's a term of endearment. His name is President X, and right now, I am an excited contestant in the Last Lady Pageant, held to determine President X's final Nancy. If you're in the West, or even overseas, that might confuse you. In East America, we're all named Nancy. Well, the women chosen for programming are named Nancy. I don't know what the others are named. I've never seen one. Well, the girls at least. I'm Nancy159. The pageant chooses his final wife. He has five others.

You might wonder why I'm in a pageant competing for such a lofty prize if I'm ugly. The answer is: I don't know! I'm a woman, not a book! No one explains things to me! I don't ask questions! I can't be seen as curious or inquisitive—two very negative attributes in a potential wife.

I suppose I have virtues other than beauty. After seven years of programming, I don't spend much time thinking at all. Becoming a Nancy doesn't happen overnight—and it's not all daisies and rose petals! My inside and outsides are genetically modified to look nearly identical to Nancy1, the prototype. We spend hours plugged into the thought machines: long, metal, tubular thrones that plug us into each other. Getting plugged into a thought machine is like meditation of the deepest kind. Nancys are like monks— we tap into a deep energy. But the energy we tap into isn't a Higher Power—it's each other. We share a mind. I am a separate Nancy, but I can dive into the pool of my sisters . . . the pool of my selves, really . . .

Look at me, prattling on! It is almost time for me to go onstage. The lights, I can't describe them, they are insane. Bright, flashing. This year's pageant is being broadcast live. Live. My hands feel tight and dry. My stomach feels empty and small. I step onto the stage and into the bright lights and smile. I can't see Them, but I can hear their applause. I feel the bottom of my bathing suit hike up, but I don't dare fix it; I mustn't move. I turn around in a slow circle. The claps grow louder.

"Nancy159, why do you think you should advance to the next round of this competition?"

The voice is booming, loud. It surprises me. I jump. The audience laughs.

I am not sure why I was chosen in the first place and I can't remember the last time someone asked me what I think. I say, "If President X desires me, I am thrilled to advance to the next round." I do not know how many rounds there are. Or what happens to the Nancys who are deemed losers. "I am obedient and well—trained, and that is all I can say for myself."

"And there you have it." The Voice from Nowhere chuckles. "Well—trained. Will you walk in a line for us, sweetheart? We need to see your gait."

I put a foot forward. And then another. I freeze. I cannot make my feet go another step.

The Voice chuckles.

Beyond the bright lights I hear the audience whispering. I see the outlines of the judges, big men in suits as always. Vomit rises in my throat. I stop and swallow it and still I cannot display my gait. This is a fault, I'm sure of it. Other faults include: physical strength, infertility, self-reliance, courage, and directness. Desired attributes include: submissiveness, helplessness, selflessness, and sexual and domestic talents.

"Not sure about this one," the Voice says. His tone has changed; I can hear a difference. "She might be a lemon." He sighs. "Shame. Genetically, she is something else. Her lineage would astound you."

What a liar he is! My mother was a nobody.

"Looks like it might have to end here, gentlemen."

Oh no. Feelings are happening. Shame and fear, deep and dark. I want so badly to sit on the ground and cover my eyes. What will I do if President X does not pick me? Who will I belong to?

The crowd grows restless. I can hear the men checking their tech, groaning.

I *cannot* lose. It could mean replacement. Or death. I have to do *something*. I open my mouth. A sound comes out. A melody. Oh dear, this is not the talent portion. There *is* no talent portion. They did away with those long ago. I do not even know any songs!

The men watching me grow silent.

Nancy6, my trainer rushes out on stage and takes my arm. "Walk and sing, 159. Walk and sing," she hisses in my ear.

I walk. I keep my head up. I keep my voice strong. I won't lose today. I can't lose today.

"Go on now. Good girl." My Beloved's voice is so near! He remembers me! He cares.

Nancy6 holds my arm in a vise—grip as I keep walking. My singing voice is earthy and low; my speaking voice is breathy and high. With training, I have mastered vocal femininity, but they do not teach us to sing. I hope my song is okay, as I cannot stop it.

I can feel the eyes of the four other Nancys in the pageant on me. They are backstage, but the odd thing is, I think I am losing my separateness. I am not used to being one me for this long. In the bright lights and all the excitement, I slip. I stop singing. I stop walking.

I close my eyes and slip from my mind into ours.

A chill comes up my spine. Our spines.

Then I hear it. The other girls singing the song of my making. They sing, like I did, in another language, a language I know they don't know. We are always able to "tap in": when they are sad, I am sad. When they are happy, I am happy. Sometimes it goes further: when Nancy63 was struck on her left arm by her Beloved last Wednesday, I felt a sharp pain in mine. I was surprised and looked around the food court. The others felt it, too. But this, this is new. One of us—me—was able to overtake all the others—when they were out of sight. Joy wells in my heart. Tears stream down my eyes. We are one, but we always feel alone. This is different.

I open my eyes. The others are no longer backstage; they are standing beside me. The song changes. It's louder, in English. It's a song I don't know. It's someone else's, but I can sing it word for word. The notes ring out clear.

I ate the apple in the garden
I spake to the serpent in the wake.
I know all the secrets
That the night keeps from the day.

I look around. We should all be voted President X's last wife. All of us: 86, 192, 184, and brand new 200. It feels wrong to differentiate. Our song goes on:

The moon ties the earth to my body.
The sky ties the heart to my sun.
And even if you have my soul
Its song cannot be won.

We smile at each other, our song echoing beyond the bright, bright lights. Only then do I realize none of our mouths are moving, a moment before the lights are cut and the sirens start.

"Make it stop!" a man screams. And then I hear many screams: "They must be reprogrammed!" and "Oh my God, what have we done?"

Large arms wrap around my waist. We are all pulled off the stage. As we are dragged away our song echoes through the auditorium and I think: it has made itself a home. I know in my heart that it will not leave without a fight.

CHAPTER 1

Avis

SEVERAL SOURCES I CONSULTED SUGGEST that if you focus on the *physical* sensation of a feeling, the *emotional* consequences will pass. I stopped taking Amplexus yesterday and it hurts in my chest, and in the tops of my eyes. I focus on the physical sensation. I remind myself: *I am a warrior. I am trained in combat. My mother is a leader of our country.* And yet I worry: *Without the pills will I be weak?* None of the writings I consulted told me about these types of thoughts. Have I made a terrible mistake? Everyone's on Amplexus in West America. Well, all the women are. It's how we came to power and it's how we Rise Above. It's gotten us past the infertility bombs, the poisoned gas, the ground attacks. The tech shutdowns. We did it with cold, hard rationalization. We did it with math. We did it with science. But also with the pills my mother invented.

I stopped taking it for training purposes. What if I were to be captured by the East? In the event of a kidnapping, I need to be prepared. I have never felt the Weaker Emotions before. I cannot let my body experience that sort of shock. This seems so logical, but yet, I must keep it a secret. Francesca would not approve.

I take a deep breath. It's time to get up. I feel something different, I can't name it but I feel the edges of it. Hot and twisted. It creeps up on me. The colors and feelings come first. The thoughts come next. *What am I doing?* flashes through my mind, an orange thought. Then *Does it matter?* appears, a deeper orange. Finally: *Why get out of bed?* is a deep red thought. I have never had thoughts in colors; I've never had low feelings like this. The drug stunts the Weaker Emotions. I started taking the pills so early I wasn't supposed to develop any of the Weaker Emotions: sadness, fear, infatuation, romantic love. Yet here I am, experiencing these things after only one missed dose. I roll out of bed and put on my thick, wire-rimmed glasses. I stare at my stone headboard and white sheets; I've never realized how boring they are. *Why should I care? Is it bad to care? What is this feeling?*

I cannot sit here and pontificate. My mother expects me at breakfast, and if I do not attend she will know something is wrong. She cannot know I quit taking the Amplexus.

I hear our houseboys making breakfast, horsing around, listening to some sort of music. I've never really paid attention to their music. I've never been much into music at all, honestly, it is so superfluous. This song is filled with strings, is my guess. I do know, though, that the popular music in W.A. (West America) is electronic. So this stuff must be from the former USA, or at least emulating it. I walk along the cold concrete floor until I catch my face in a mirror. I stop. I'm short. I'm lumpy. My dark, coarse hair sticks up in the back, curls in the front. My caramel skin is covered in dark freckles. I'm wearing a pair of black cotton shorts and a maroon tunic. *I look like . . . I look like . . .* I don't know. I have no simile. I don't look like my mother: she is the most beautiful woman in West America. I do know that whatever this feeling is, it's in my spine, and my eyebrows . . . it's a bit of a flush. It is akin to what I've read of Shame, but not quite. *Insecurity?* My Goddess.

I head down the hall through the sprawling ranch, listening to the houseboys' music. These banjos (I think?) sound pretty great. Very different. There seems to be no message—no political lesson on the power of womanhood. That's what's popular now, some instruction set to house music with bombs going off in the background. A recording of the Moth Twins clicking over ominous electronic beats. I've heard there's a mix of stuff my mother has said in speeches that's all the rage. She says they play it at dance clubs; I find that hard to believe. Though who knows? I've never been to a dance club. Not allowed. This banjo music, it sounds . . . lazy. Happy. I close my eyes. I feel it: it's blue, then yellow. I dance by myself in the hall for a couple of minutes, letting these new sensations wash over me.

"Hey Princess."

I feel a tap on my shoulder and my immediate instinct is to strike, but since I am in my own home I turn around first, crouched to attack. It's only a houseboy.

"Oh, hello Ethan." I hear my heart pounding in my chest. I feel blood rushing through my veins. *Perhaps this is . . . intuition?* I've read about that. Maybe my body is telling me that Ethan is a spy. Or a thief.

"Were you going to hit me just now?"

"Only if you were an enemy. What do you need?" I've got to sit down, I'm feeling *odd*.

"Well, I come in peace. Here, you dropped these."

My glasses fell off in the process of whirling around to attack him. Bile rises in my throat. I take a deep breath. I am coming off a very strong medication, and nausea is to be expected, I am sure.

"Avis, are you okay?"

I stand up straight, to show composure. "Yes." No. I feel faint.

"Did you hear about what's happened in East America? It's *all over* the tech," Ethan says, oblivious to my discomfort.

"Is that your banjo playing?" I ask. "I rather like it."

"It's a recording. Are you sure you're okay?"

Am I nodding? I nod.

He turns and yells down the stairs. "Did you hear that, boys? Avis Baron likes my bluegrass!"

The boys whoop and giggle. I don't care what a bunch of men think, but I know they would not act so ridiculous in front of my mother, Francesca. I should punish them, but I feel light-headed and need something to eat. Ethan walks away from me, and I relax. East America? What is he talking about? I note that the grey-green, tattered shirt he's wearing is getting too small for him; I can see the lean lines of his torso through the fabric. *Why do I care what he's wearing?* "Ethan—"

He whirls back around to face me, light on his bare feet. In slow motion, I see Ethan run his hand through his curly brown hair and open his mouth to speak. I've never noticed his hair before. He's in the sun so pieces of it are golden . . . that's rare these days. His tone is warm and I see the burnt sienna color of his voice as he says, "Avis, I made waffles."

Waffles. What a beautiful word. I run up the creaky fortress stairs until I burst into the kitchen, panting. "Ethan made waffles? And I like these banjos!"

She stares at me, agog. She walks toward me quickly and takes my face in her hands, taking stock of my pupils. Her hands are rough, torn up, hardened. They look as if she's been building a bomb. Perhaps she has.

"Did you take your Amplexus?"

"I took it!" I lie. I sit on our giant wooden table—an ancient thing from before the war. "Last night, as always."

She looks relieved. She comes over to sit next to me. We have a nice house. It's sort of a bunker, but only half of it is underground, so we can still call it a house.

"You've got to take it every day. You don't want to lose your bearings, Avis." She touches my hair. "You're growing into yourself, you know." Houseboys buzz around us, trying to be silent. They still whisper, hum. We have not been strict enough with them.

We turn and face a large mirror, framed in sea glass.

"I look like a Moth Twin."

"You shouldn't call them that. It's a tragedy what happened to those women."

The Moth Twins were born sixteen years ago after the infertility attacks. President X flooded our water with Zansbosin, a toxin that causes infertility in women. Their mother was poisoned, but somehow they developed to term. They were born transparent, with segmented limbs. They speak mostly in clicks, and only to each other; if you give them a tech they can spell out what they want with their spidery fingers. We call them the Moth Twins not due to their appearance, but because they eat bugs. They were in my second-grade class, and I saw Beneeva, the slightly larger one, eat two pencil erasers, an ant, an old raisin she found on the floor, a moth, and four mosquitoes.

My mother laughs. "You know, I looked just like you when I was your age. Give it time. It doesn't matter what you look like, but know that you *will* look different." She sighs. "I dread it. I don't know why." She changes the subject. "Do you know where Thaddeus is?"

Thaddeus is thirty-seven, a houseboy, and my mom's right hand. He's brilliant and not cis-gendered, which gives him more value. He's also my nanny. I do not know where he is. Ethan pops back into my mind and I ask, "Mom, what's going on in East America?"

"What are you talking about?" Anger colors her voice red. She's upset.

"I heard something on the tech," I lie. My second. *So this is what lying is like.*

"We don't have any of those channels," she counters. Then she relents. "President X is picking his last wife. His demand for younger and younger Nancys means that he's . . . choosing from women who have not . . . been through the entire program, is the best way to put it."

I wait for her to say more. This is nothing new. President X has held a pageant to pick a "final" wife three times already after the original two. I'm not convinced of the validity of the contest.

"There were some . . . issues at the pageant. It's raised some alarms. Our allies and I—we think the Nancys might have more of their authentic selves left than we originally thought. More than we thought could survive the Programming."

I consider this. "What about us? Do you think Amplexus takes away from our authentic selves?" I've wondered this for ages.

"Absolutely not! What a question, Avis. You know better than most that emotions and lust prevent us from obtaining our desires. You can feel what you want. You have passion. What is it you want, Avis?"

By rote I answer: "To defeat President X and free the women of North America."

"That's my girl."

"But do you remember all the drug addiction in the Old States? All the pills that they thought would help them? People died, people lost their patriarchal families." I have never questioned her before so blatantly. It tingles in my eyes and in my armpits.

"Those people were weak. Those people were seeking oblivion."

"There were drugs that made you better, as well. I've read about them, Mother. Beta-blockers. Adderall."

"Avis, honestly. Talking about the past gives us nothing. Let's look towards the future."

If I didn't know any better, I'd call the face she's making "worry." "Can I see a replay of the event in the East?"

"Later."

There is a different color in her voice. It's green now. She's always been secretive about her feelings, and about the past. About science-related things. But never about current events. This is curious. I could ask Ethan to give me the details of what happened at the pageant, but there are recording devices all over the house, so I will have to make a plan.

It won't be the first time I've acted behind Francesca's back.

CHAPTER 2

Thaddeus

THE DUSTY STREETS OF NEW SANTA FE aren't the safest place for men right now, but people know who I am. It's December, but it's still pretty hot. There are no seasons after the environmental attacks of the late 2020s, but tonight is especially arid at 81 degrees. I walk every night. To me, West America looks like an abandoned mining town from the ancient cowboy movies I watched as a child. Forty-six years of war have destroyed this place. I look at the broken streetlights. Men on street corners. I see a gaggle of little girls playing with toy guns in the road. They shouldn't be in the road. But the danger is minimal; not many people can afford a vehicle. This evening, I walk until I find myself along a chain—link fence on the outside of the Stacks, a community made of shipping containers.

A light's on in a red container window, and I can see a woman and her partner. I'm guessing he's her partner; in the Stacks, you're allowed to have a partner. Mainly because there is no room for houseboys. Intercourse outside of procreation is still forbidden, of course. Her partner brings her roasted vegetables and grains on stone plates. We haven't had meat in New Santa Fe for years; the twin problems of obesity and pollution were so severe after the infertility strike that the government outlawed half the grocery. The man takes his own plate and leaves the room. In a few seconds he's outside. He nods to me and lights up a cigarette.

"I know you. You're on the tech. You work for Francesca."

I nod. He offers me a cigarette and I take it. I haven't seen one in a while; he must know someone. Or she does. Probably her.

"Did you eat your food?"

He nods no.

"Not hungry?" I don't expect him to talk to me. But hey, you never know.

"I raised my son to survive," he tells me, after taking a long drag. "She wants me to give him to a rich family. So they can partner him off to some girl or use him as a worker. Whatever they decide." His voice sounds crackly, gravelly. Like he hasn't used it in months. "She thinks a male child divides her loyalties to the party. That he is 'emotionally distracting.' I wish I could've given her a daughter."

"Times change," I tell him. They always do.

"Listen, brother. Have you seen that video of the Nancys? If President X's women are breaking he's gonna want new ones, and we're—"

"What video?"

He looks at me like I am simple. Then he taps his wrist. His tech appears before us, a square, translucent screen. I see a video of a horse running through a field.

"Wrong video," he says, tapping his wrist again quickly, embarrassed. "That's a memory."

"It's beautiful," I say, because it is. "No worries."

He brings up a new segment. I immediately recognize a Last Lady Pageant. I see a young girl on stage. She looks frozen and then . . . then there is singing. *Oh shit.*

"What's wrong?" he asks.

"She's only a child. And she . . . she . . . she looks familiar. They can change their outsides—but her face—"

"Do you think Francesca will stop him?" He makes a hopeless gesture with his free hand.

"It'll be okay," I assure him. Platitudes are all I have right now.

He nods. He puts out his cigarette and goes inside without another word. I don't think this cigarette man will last long in the West. Every day there are men lining up at the border to the East. They all have similar stories: their partners have left them, they have nowhere to go, and no currency. The job market's bad, and no one's going to hire a man. Not unless they want someone to teach or watch their kids, and barely anyone's having kids these days.

I was born and raised in the East. I know that it's filled with ideas so poison you have to turn on all the lights and shut your brain just to keep them out.

I look toward the red stacker the man disappeared into. He could join the armed forces; a lot of them do. But I don't think he'd be a success. The women push harder, and without a synthetic like Amplexus men just can't keep up with them. If he joins he'll likely be ridiculed, perhaps beaten. Amplexus gives women mental and physical strength that is formidable. I remember how nervous my mother used to be. How afraid she was for me and my sister. No woman is like that anymore.

Desperate times call for desperate measures, we tell ourselves. I wonder if all our fighting about population and gender rights is in vain. Maybe there truly is some higher being? A being that will tell us we've all taken a wrong turn. I finish my cigarette. Hell, I think. Maybe a bunch of aliens will land and tell us the truth: we've taken the wrong path. Or squash us like bugs. Or not care about us at all, the way we feel when a fish eats its young.

Francesca'll be mad at me for being gone for so long. She hasn't accepted that Avis is sixteen and doesn't need me at every moment.

I come up to the house. For a land run by women, you'd think they'd have taste. It's a log cabin sort of structure on the top that holds the houseboys, the storage. Avis's treehouse juts out from behind it. Everything else is underground. She's too old for that thing, but I know she needs the privacy. Can't keep secrets here. The bunker's underground. I walk up in between two cacti and tap my foot on the metal door. I back up. It opens.

I walk down the creaky stairs, to check on Avis, and that's when I hear it. My spine tingles from top to bottom as I listen to a song I haven't heard in fifteen years.

The moon ties the earth to my body.

The sky ties the heart to my sun.

And even if you have my soul

Its song cannot be won

Francesca's parents were from the old country. And I don't mean the Old States—I mean where the Far East used to be. Her mother sang her a song, passed down from generations. So she'd sing to Avis, in Arabic, when she was a baby. Before the uprising. Before she hid who she was. Before any of this. The song changes. The timbre of Avis's voice changes. It's as if it's not her at all.

I head in to her room. "Avis, what are you singing?" I hope I sound calmer than I feel. "How do you know that song?"

"I wasn't singing." She looks astonished that I'd suggest such a thing.

"Yes you were. I heard you on the stairs. Did you hear that on your tech?"

"I don't know. I wasn't singing, Thaddeus. I was just humming some song. What's happening in the East? Please do not lie to me."

She looks—upset.

"Why do you care?" I wonder.

"I feel for those women. I worry about them. What their lives must be like, like that. Dead inside."

A tear wells in her eye.

"Shit, Avis! You can't just stop taking your Amplexus! What is wrong with you?"

She hides her face. She cries. I hold her, like I used to. Before she started taking the drugs. When she still needed me.

"If I get kidnapped, and I don't have my pills—I have to know how to function."

She's got a point.

"Where are the pills? You can't flush them. They'll get in the water supply. Do you know what that could do to the houseboys?"

She throws a bottle of pills at me like a petulant child and flops back on her bed.

"The East. Tell me!"

"The Nancys—one of them sang. Then—I don't know exactly, their minds joined and they sang together. I am not sure what happened, but their programming is whack for sure."

"Could it be a good thing?"

"Maybe," I lie. I haven't believed in good things in a long time.

CHAPTER 3

Nancy159

"WELCOME TO THE NICE ROOM for Mean Things," Nancy40 says.

Due to the incident in the first round, the second part of the Last Lady Pageant is no longer going to be televised. The other girls spend a lot of time worrying—about what the public will think, about how we were pulled off the stage. If there will be harsher punishments. I have but one worry: my beloved President X. In Round 2, current wives interview each contestant, one on one. You are expected to talk about yourself, out loud. It will still be filmed by President X's staff—everything President X does is, it is history. This part of the competition is not where you prove you can get along with the other wives; that's to be expected. Instead, it's imperative that you prove to them that you are up to par. They are so well-trained, so perfectly programmed, and they expect the same from you. There must be no more surprises. My song was a surprise. I have not yet been caned. Perhaps they like singing. Music is popular among men, I hear. I try not to dwell on it, I have already vomited four times today.

We share a Hive-Mind, but there are ways to hide. The wives can sniff these secrets places out. It has been three days since Round 1 and we went back to the Residence—a large, clean, white building with our little pods all in a row, perfect flowerpots for us to become perfect specimens in. We learned in design they are based after Japanese hotels! How funny, Japan. Here in East America! We really are the Center of the World! Everything is there—the tennis court, the food court, the hair salon, the thought machines. There is even a media room with appropriate media. And the closets. Oh, the closets. You wouldn't believe it. To have dozens of roommates, all in your size, all happy to share. I am so lucky.

X's Nancys live in the Old White House. Until today I've only seen it in pictures. But in person: it's everything. It has history. Finishings. Marble. Beams. Columns everywhere. Every window is different. The wainscoting. Oh, the wainscoting. It is the same design, basically, as the Old White House. Parts were unable to be repaired after the bombings and the fires, so the East Wing is burnt, and sort of flat at the top. They left it there. As a reminder to us. Of who our enemy is.

I have a new trainer, Nancy18. After the little singing incident, I never saw Nancy6 again. I've asked where she is, but I can feel the walls in the minds of my sisters go up. Maybe they didn't like her. Nancy18 is fine, I guess. Quiet. If I didn't know better, by the way she is acting and the physical I'd think Nancy18 is scared of me! But that's crazy—she must just be hormonal. We walk through many portrait-lined hallways until we reach the wives' quarters; they live separately from the men on President X's staff. Nancy6, before she was taken, told me: "A great deal of precaution is taken to make sure no one beside the Nancys and President X can enter. At the entrance to the quarters, the large metal doors open and for a moment all I see is pink: fluffy pink curtains tied with darker pink bows, plush pink carpeting on the floor. The walls are wallpapered pink and gold in a subtle damask pattern, and pink velvet "conversation couches" snake through the giant room. The furniture dates to the 1960s and '70s in the former US—I learned this in Design, my favorite class during programming. My eyes are drawn to the "conversation pit," a recessed seating area. It is circular, it is gold, and it is in the middle of the room. It has fluffy white fur pillows, and its floor appears to be made of real gold. The wives are all seated, in wait for me.

"Sit down," says 129, his most recent bride.

I sit. I look at Nancy3, Nancy40, Nancy63, Nancy97. They are all stunningly beautiful. They wear their numbers on their lapels, tiny gold pins, but eventually I will be able to tell them apart. The hair is a slightly different texture. The eyes have slightly different shapes. Some breasts are natural, others not. We all look the same—but only to a point. We learned in Makeup—"Your eyebrows are sisters, not twins!" It's the same with us. Sisters, not twins.

40 nods. 63 smiles. 97 examines her nails. 3 doesn't look up from her knitting.

"You were a Black, were you not? Your bleaching took better than I'd expected. Do you have to keep up with it?" 40 asks.

"A Brown. Unsure what kind. The bleach took, though! I still can't go in the sun. Nothing a parasol can't fix." It hurt a lot. It still hurts. I was brown. I'm white now. Most of the body modifications they gave me hurt but I won't tell them that; I don't want to sound ungrateful for what's been given to me. I know how ugly I was in my true form.

They titter with laughter, except for 3. She's still stuck in her knitting. Then, they go quiet. I know what's coming.

129 turns to 3. "Nancy3, after that—horrible display on stage—I feel like we're not all on the same page. Shall we breathe together?"

"No!" 40 says immediately. "I don't want to take her in. We've seen she's terrible."

"Positive moods overpower negative ones!" 129 recites. "We'll be fine!"

All the Nancys murmur agreement except 97.

"97 is mute," 129 explains.

I look at 97; she stands and approaches me. I am surprised when she takes my face in her hand.

"Yes," says 3, with a touch of impatience. "She is pretty." 3 turns to me and says, "97 is so shallow." Then she addresses the other wives. "Let's do this."

She wants to recalibrate. They take a deep breath together.

"Close your eyes, Nancy159," she says to me. "We need you to keep yourself."

I close my eyes and hold my breath. Recalibrating seems crazy when you first hear of it, but women have always been in tune with one another's needs. When women live in a house together, their moon cycles match up—that's a fact from always, not from programming. We've always been many and one; our programming just makes us better.

Anyway, recalibrating: we do it when one of us is in a bad mood. Occasionally, though, and especially with a very well-programmed Nancy—and Nancy3 is first generation, they programmed the first batch the most carefully, women were much more rebellious then, many were Western—the bad mood can spread instead and ruin everyone's afternoon.

"Open your eyes." They all speak at once.

"Wow," I say, surprised. "You are very in sync."

"You shouldn't sound so surprised," 129 says. "We saw your little song."

"As you may imagine," 63 says, "we were pleased to see all the contestant Nancys come together in song, but not pleased—"

"That you think *you* are important enough to take over everyone else," finishes 3. "Please explain yourself."

I think 40 was right about not recalibrating: Nancy3's mood has claimed them all.

"I didn't take over," I say. "I don't even know those songs," I add.

"The first song was from your childhood," 3 says.

"We looked through your archives," adds 40. "We saw your mother sing it to you both."

Sing it to us both? Archives are only for important people.

"You do not know who you are, we can see." 63 hands me a glass filled with a pink, bubbly drink.

"This is the Nice Room for Mean Things," 129 says, repeating what 40 had said.

"Do you know why we have this interview? Why it is part of the pageant?" asks 3.

"To serve our Beloved, President X," I say, holding my fizzing drink.

"To serve our Beloved, yes. But also, there have been infiltrators," says 129. "We have met women who are broken—in spirit and in thought. Some of them we sent back for refinishing. Some of them were executed after their time in this room."

I put down my glass.

"We'd hate to do that," says 63. "Still, we have to know, are you for the West? Or are you with us?"

"If you are programmed incorrectly, we could lose—"

"I'm not for the West!"

"You say that. But we don't want to deal with another 86."

They all agree wholeheartedly.

"Try me," I say. I know what happened to 86. Two years ago, a Nancy was poorly trained and wanted to write a book about her experience. To sell it to the West. Her body is preserved in the Square of the Residence in a glass box. They taxidermied her, sewed buttons on her eyes as a message. "Recalibrate with me."

They nod. We hold hands. I look at their eyes. All the same perfect shade of blue, thanks to science. They look at mine. They breathe me in. I breathe me out.

I picture pansies to add bubble to my personality. I picture a kitten to add cuteness.

3 takes her hands away and laughs. "She's harmless! So submissive! And from her family—how can this be? He *should* pick her."

"I see how sweet and calm she is," agrees 129. "But it's too early to choose. We still have three more Nancys to interview.

"Excuse me, ladies," I say, making myself look both happy and bashful. "Where is the powder room?"

"In there, behind the steel wall," says 3, in a warm tone. "We don't like to feel each other's bowel movements."

They all giggle. They've caught my bubbly personality. Unfortunately, I've caught something else. I walk slowly toward the bathroom. I hear them in conversation with on another, and I now they're not paying attention to the me in my body but the me in their heads. I enter the restroom and lock the door. The room is yellow flowered, and looks like the American 1960s I've seen in textbooks. It's beautiful. I look into the mirror and into my own eyes. Tears well in them. *This is a steel room,* I remind myself. *They can't feel me. They can't hear me.*

I can remember. I can remember things from before my programming.

I remember my mother, her dark skin and maroon hair. I remember my old eyes—brown and soulful. And there's something else. It's at the corner of my thoughts. It's something they know and I don't. 129 was trying to tell me. Or maybe it was 3? While we were recalibrating one of them passed a phrase to me on purpose: "You were two." I look in the mirror. Two years old? What does it mean? I wipe my tears and smile. I am so close to winning, so close to having a dream status in society. "You were two." Who gave these words to me? Which one of them? How curious.

CHAPTER 4

Avis

IT'S BEEN TWO DAYS SINCE my last dose of
Amplexus. My physical skills are still up to par, but I find
that my interests have changed, and my emotions are
intense. I have a treehouse near the fortress—my mother
said "a young woman should always have a place to go be
alone with her thoughts." So here I am, where I used to
play as a child, with an old, square music player and some
music of my mom's from the aughts. I've never cared for
music and now it's like I can *feel* the notes in my whole
body. Past my body, even, to somewhere else. Everything
tingles. I'm not convinced this is due to withdrawal.

I decorated this tree house years ago with propaganda
from my mom's political career. Some of the posters I

took from the house, some of them I made myself, using the slogans I heard over and over. In crayon, as an eight-year-old, I scribbled "ABOLISH THE NUCLEAR FAMILY," and "SEX BENDS THE FEMALE MIND AND CORRUPTS THE FEMALE BODY."

I hear footsteps; I grab a bat and look outside. A good side effect of stopping Amplexus—I have become *quite* vigilant. It's just Ethan. He's still wearing that goddess-awful shirt. I should request my mother to buy him another, it is her duty. "Ethan? Come join me," I call down to him.

He stares at me for a second. Then he climbs the ladder. His grin tilts to one side and I notice that I feel warm all over, especially my face and stomach. Maybe I am experiencing withdrawal?

"What is it? Do you have orders for me, Princess?"

"Don't talk so loud," I hiss. His grin grows even more lopsided; is he doing that on purpose? "And don't call me that."

"What else would I call you?"

I ignore this foolish question and get straight to my point. "I want to know more about this thing with the Nancys."

"I was wondering when you would get curious about things; it's not like your mother can—"

"It's weird that I'm talking to you," I blurt. "A houseboy. A male."

"I'm a person. We could be friends."

I laugh. Then I consider it; I have never had a friend before. But friends with a male? I don't know. "Who are you friends with?" I ask, stalling, considering my options.

"The other guys. My dog."

Yes. That is appropriate. "You can be my friend like a dog. Sit."

He laughs. He sits. He thinks I am being funny.

"Stay."

He doesn't move.

"Good boy," I say and joy fills my body like a cold glass of water. I pat his head. I've always liked dogs. "Nancys. Tell me."

"Pat my head again."

I do. I've never touched him before and he's relishing this.

"You should be scared of me," I remind him, in a whisper. "Most of the houseboys won't even look at me."

"I look at you all the time."

I get the music box. "I'm going to play you something. It's an old music." I sit on the ground, near him. I play the song. He sings along—

His voice is golden with hints of brown and parts that are forest green. The music makes me float above my body . . . when the song ends I realize he's holding my hand, and tears are streaming down my cheeks. Tears stream down his cheeks, too.

"You stopped taking that pill," he says. It isn't a question.

"I want to be a warrior without it," I say. It is only part of the truth, but it is true. Then I say, "Ethan, in this moment I have feelings for you that concern me."

"Are you mad at me? I'm sorry—"

"I'm not mad. Perhaps it is just comradery. Yet I think my feelings *could* be romantic in nature, and possibly sexual—"

He stands up. He wipes his hands on his jeans. "Don't fire me," he says. "I'll get deported to the East. Killed maybe!"

I jump up. "I won't! I mean it's not like I would—"

"You should take your Amplexus again," he says.

"I don't know, Ethan; I've never had these feelings before. It's like I'm made of cold fire . . ."

And then his mouth is on mine. My eyes widen in surprise, but I do not move my head. He kisses my mouth, my forehead, my nose, my eyebrows. My cheeks.

"We could be killed for this," he states. "Is that a risk you want to take?"

A minute ago I would have said no. "Why is it so bad?" I ask him, though I know.

"Because people of my sex used to make people of your sex scared all the time," he feeds me the answer. "And I don't want you to be scared," he adds.

"I'm not scared of you!" I swear. I could easily take him in combat, I am certain of it.

"That power and confidence you feel now," he says. "Everyone knows that once you're in love, you lose it. You lose the wholeness and power of yourself."

"I wouldn't."

"*Everyone* does."

I take a deep breath. "I love you," I declare. I saw it in a movie once; I heard it in a song. I know the words. But these feelings make me certain they live in my body now.

"You don't know what that means."

"I'm feeling—"

"It's not a feeling in your body. Love is—it's an action. It's what you do every day when you care about someone. You don't love me. You and I can be comrades. Friends. I'm your dog, remember?"

"People love their dogs," I say, stubbornly.

"I have to tell you something, Avis. And I only tell you this because I have feelings for you, too; I have for a long time." He brings up his tech; he brightens it so I can see the image. He shows me the video of the latest Last Lady Pageant. I watch the Nancys breaking into song. Then the video cuts to a newscaster who discusses what this could potentially mean.

"What you are seeing here may seem like a performance, but is more like a psychotic break. X is ignoring it, chalking it up to a bad handler—but we never knew the Hive-Mind was so strong—look at them—if you look closely, as we zoom in here—they are inhaling and exhaling at the same time. They have all become one." The newscaster herself looks terrified, yet exhilarated.

My mother was right! Perhaps the women of East America are not as gone as we once thought. I'm about to share this thought with Ethan when he pauses on a single Nancy. He makes the picture bigger.

"Look at her," he says to me.

I look at her. She looks so familiar. I touch my own face. I touch my own hair.

"They bleach them, you know. Their skin. Their hair."

"I don't understand," I whisper. "I think I know her." *How can that be?*

Darkness and doubt swirls through my body, coloring my words dark and smoky. For the first time, I regret not taking my Amplexus.

"How long have we known each other, Avis?"

"Since forever."

"I came here when I was four. You were two. There was another girl here. Another baby. Your mother won't speak of her—I asked her once and she nearly fired me. I always thought she died—but the nose—the mouth—her voice, my Goddess, her *voice.*"

"What are you saying, Ethan?"

"I think this is your sister."

CHAPTER 5

Thaddeus

SOMETHING'S GOING ON WITH THE NANCYS.
My sister, Nyx, is a Nancy. It's not uncommon. I went
with her to her skin bleaching appointments in East Old
Boston when she was first accepted to Finishing Camp.
Her excitement as her skin turned lighter—they used
lasers and tinctures and everything you can possibly
imagine—was a real surprise to me. I guess it shouldn't
have been; even in "post-racial" times, the second shit hits
the fan the first thing men want is light eyes and pale skin.
White skin is a real uncommon thing nowadays, at least, as
a natural occurrence. It was pretty much bred out. It's rare,
so maybe that's why it is coveted.

My mother and I visited Nyx as she went through
Phase 1. It was hard: we watched her forget her name,

we watched her hilarious, sarcastic personality replaced by something different, something false.

I was eight the last time I saw her. The soon-to-be Nancys were all playing tennis that day. We were at the Residence, where they live and train. I was a child, but already I knew it was important for women to keep up their figures. And to be good enough at sports to be entertaining without being too challenging to men. I watched dozens of courts. On each smooth layer of green asphalt I watched blonde women smashing balls. I listened to them giggle like they were having the best time ever. Even at eight, I realized there was something wrong—something grotesque—with what I was watching. The balls flew, the rackets thwacked, and when I realized what I was truly witnessing I started to scream. The balls bounced, the rackets thwacked, the women panted, all in *perfect* unison, *at the exact same time.*

My sister didn't acknowledge my screams. None of them did. White skirts and whittled waists, not a drop of sweat among them: they all kept playing. I've never forgotten that day. I vowed never to become a Nancy and to go west as soon as I was old enough. And I did. I escaped. And I do my best to keep my past locked in a memory room that I rarely visit, but today it is all flooding back, because I have received a message from my sister Krista. I've read it countless times already. She must have paid a considerable amount of money to get this letter over. When I think of what she did to make it, I shudder.

Seaview Hospital
4th Quadrant, East America
URGENT

Thad,

It's me. Don't freak out. I know you must be surprised to hear from me, but this is the first chance I have had at untapped tech. I saw a picture of you in a ticker, sitting next to Francesca Baron. I couldn't believe it was you. You're a man now!

I don't have much time, but I need you to know: The Nancy training doesn't stick for everyone. There is a glitch in the system. Some women get sent back to be re-finished. Some women's guys let it slide. Mine doesn't know. I dust the same shit over and over, look nice, and laugh at his dumb jokes and that kept him happy for a long time.

The trouble started when I was reading while Roy was away. He left his library unlocked—he doesn't know I can read. I found a book called the Brisbane Boy. Have you read it? It is about a queen in England, Queen Elizabeth I. She was so powerful everyone thought she must be a man. The book made me think of you. ☺ It's a history book, a conspiracy one, but I believe that old thoughts can become new again, because things started to come back to me. Memories. When Roy returned and I was being sexed, I could not hold perfectly still. I started screaming. I couldn't stop. I remembered.

So Roy said he didn't want me anymore. Agents came and put me in a tiny hospital room. It's where I am now. There's nowhere for me to go from here with that screaming incident on my record besides home delivery sex services. I'd rather saw off my own head with a nail file.

So that's why I've contacted you. I've arranged to cross the border ASAP. I can work for you and Francesca. I have excellent manners; I am trained in child rearing, pleasantries, and several forms of dance (including soft shoe and dressage). It has not been determined if I'm barren from the attacks, so I am valuable on that front, even out West. Will you help me? The info you need should be on your tech.

Yours now more than ever,
Your big sister, Krista

Good Goddess. I have not seen Krista since I was ten years old. I take a deep breath and open the vial of pills I stole from Avis's room immediately after I received

Krista's message. She's not taking them anymore and I've always been curious about them. I'm not an idiot; I know they may not work for me, but I'm willing to try. Courage is a virtue: Amplexus makes you more courageous, and harboring a fugitive Nancy requires bravery. It is not business as usual. The penalty, for most, is to be put in a labor camp. I wonder if I could hide her in the upper level of the house. Francesca hasn't been leaving her lab much, let alone going above ground. It's going to be risky, very risky. And if I get Francesca involved? It will be damn near chaotic.

I don't know how to contain my emotions. I feel so happy, so scared, all at the same time. I am going to see my sister again! And then I feel mortified by the faraway quality of her words, the way she values herself by the garbage they filled her with.

First those contestants singing and now this. The women in the Eastern Hemisphere are getting rowdy. I can *feel* it. They are finally screaming. Francesca will say that they are readying themselves to rise in vengeance for the hangings in Salem and the rapes in Nanking all the way back to the rape of the Sabines. She will go further back, and say that all women are tired of being punished for a girl eating an apple in a garden an eon ago.

I have a shorter view. I say their cries are for the silence of their mothers, and their mothers before them.

CHAPTER 6

Nancy159

THE OVAL OFFICE IS FULL of rats. Apparently. I overheard Nancy18 say there's been rats in it for hundreds of years; it's a very old building. For this third round of the pageant, I have a dinner with President X, alone. I've never been alone with him before; we contestants have only spoken to him as a group. That happened when he came backstage during the first round of the pageant, to watch us change into our swimwear. I am nervous, because although the wives seemed to like me, what if they like another contestant better? Would they tell him their opinion? Does he care what they think? Could I lose? My life would be over. I am being quite literal. I have never seen a Nancy that lost a Lady's Pageant afterwards. I don't *know* that they are dead, but it would make sense. Of what use are they to us now?

This round, there is only a digital camera set up—no crew. I've been instructed to wait in the hall until further instruction. So I'm standing here, looking for rattraps. A robotic voice startles me: "Action!"

I open the door to the Oval Office and step inside. The first thing I see is the East American flag. It hangs above a large desk. It is red with our country's motto emblazoned on it in white script: A LEARNED WOMAN BRINGS A MAN'S DARK PREDILECTIONS TO LIGHT. Seeing something so familiar calms me.

"This is what you picked to wear? To the Oval Office?"

"I was styled by your wives," I say. President X's voice is very deep; it rings through the room. Immediately I reconsider my answer; I do not want to contradict him. "I will wear whatever you want me to," I say.

"Take it off," he demands.

I step out of the modest black dress, a vintage piece more beautiful than any I have ever touched. Black lace underwear and a bra is all I have on.

"Take that off, too."

I take off my bra. I start to take off my underwear, and he groans.

"Not your panties. You're in the Oval Office. Have some respect."

He indicates a chair and I sit down.

A man appears out of nowhere and pours me wine. I have never had wine. In training, they teach us about different wine, pairings, and so forth, but they do not give it to us. We stick to water or seltzer—anything else has too many calories. There are also steak and potatoes. I've never had steak. Potatoes, I'm familiar with those.

"I'd like to see you demonstrate your conversational skills."

I think this could be a trick; a Nancy is supposed to be a good listener, a shoulder to cry on, but a conversationalist— that implies I have something to say. This implication challenges me.

"My conversational skills." I say. "I am sixteen." I do not know how old X is, fifty at least. "Sir, my interest in you is . . . " I search for the most acceptable response. "It is a lot. It is the most. It is the best interest." I hold my breath hoping he is pleased.

"Good start, my dear. Have some wine."

He points to my glass and I drink. It tastes terrible. I do not let my reaction show. I'm sitting topless with the president of the Eastern States. And it is nice, because I'm in a place where no Nancys can feel me, can know what my inner thoughts are. For the first time in as long as I can remember.

"Eat some steak."

I do. It tastes like I'd imagine my own tongue would taste if I cut it off and fried it. This is neither a good or a bad thing. As I chew, I devise a way to rise myself above the other contestants in his esteem. I am the youngest. I have that at least.

"President X, you are so marvelous; what are your plans for East America? I want to know."

He makes a face, as I hoped he would. "It's not appropriate for Nancys to have political interests."

"Oh, my Beloved!" I say. "My interests aren't political. They are only in you."

He smiles, pleased. I have pleased him. I take a deep sip of my wine.

"I like you—what number are you, again?"

"159."

"Well, 159, I am going to make this country great. I am going to create a traditional, beautiful place. Like Old America. Where everyone knew their place. In Old America everyone was happy. Are you happy, 159?"

"I am." Right now I am.

He pours me more wine. "Looking at you now, I have decided you are not as ugly as I once thought. Many told me to eliminate you after the singing incident, but I enjoyed your song. I think the Nancys should be taught music; my colleagues think it is too dangerous, could be a method of rebellion, one of the few things we are divided on. But I liked your voice, and my opinion matters most."

"Thank you so much."

"Eat some more steak."

I take a bite. He reaches over and touches my breast, as if he's examining a vegetable in a store bin, determining if it is ripe.

"Real?"

"No." I chew. "They are part of my reconstruction."

"I see. They do great work."

"They use real fat cells."

"Cameras off. Sounds off," X commands. "How do you feel about me touching your breast. Do not lie. I want the truth."

I stop chewing. I take a drink of wine. I think about the truth. "Well, my Beloved, I would be honored to marry you. I think the truth is this: when I was very young, I was hit in the nose during a dance class. I did not expect such contact and I called the little girl that did the worst word I had ever heard."

"What was that word?"

I can see that I have amazed him, that this is not an answer he anticipated. I feel light. I almost feel free. "I called her a motherfucker."

There is pure silence in the room. And then I hear President X unbutton his pants. "And that's how you felt when I touched your breast?" he says in whisper. "That I am a motherfucker?"

"Sir, that's the last time I had the feeling I had when you were handling," and now I touch it myself, "my breast."

President X begins doing something under the table. I think it is sexual. I feel nothing.

"159, I want you to call me a motherfucker."

I do. I call him a motherfucker again. And again. Until he stops whatever he's doing under the table and sighs. He takes my napkin and brings it under the table. Then he tosses it on the table and stands. "Put your dress back on. Do not tell my wives about this. You bring me a special pleasure. You are through to Round 4."

I have my dress halfway up already as I say, "Thank you for dinner, sir."

He touches my breast again. I look him dead in the face and smile wide. He groans. I pull up my dress, zip it, and walk out. Thank God. I am through to Round 4.

CHAPTER 7

Avis

I FOUND HER FIRST IN my treehouse.

She was hiding in there, just sitting. Not doing anything—just sitting by herself.

My intuition is stronger than it was, I now believe Amplexus dampens it. I felt her presence while I was on the ladder, going up. My heart rate quickened, but I climbed the ladder quickly, going right toward my fear, as my mother says we all should, and the second I saw her face I was no longer afraid.

I'd never seen a Nancy up close before. I know what they do to them is horrible—but the craftsmanship, the work that goes into creating every one. How much they all look like the original—some movie actress who died young and people idolized—is uncanny. They don't change the whole face—but enough. This one though, this Nancy hiding in my treehouse, her eyes were not like theirs. They were not filled with rhetoric and false teachings like they are when they are in training, or with complete emptiness like they are later in life. Her eyes are filled with her own thoughts. And they have a familiarity to them. As if I've seen them before.

"Hello, I'm Nan—Krista. I am Krista," she says, placidly.

"How did you get here?" I whisper.

"I climbed the ladder."

"I mean—to West America. To this house. Are you on the run?"

"No, I'm just sitting. Are you Avis?"

"Yes. Are you a spy?"

"No. Though that sounds very romantic. I'm a good girl. Or I used to be. I'm Thad's sister."

I hear footsteps outside. Then I hear Thad on the ladder. His head pops up.

"Oh Avis, this is not good."

"It's fine," I reply. "Can I ask you some questions?"

"Sure," she says.

"How many Nancys are there?"

"There are 250 that I know of; I'm sure they're training up more, but it takes a lot of time and money," says Krista.

"And the rest of the women in the East," I prod.

"The rest? They act like Nancys. Well, they do their best. But they *must* keep their real names. If they're pretty enough and worthy enough to get married they do—since otherwise, they're a drain on their family, the economy."

"What about work camps?" I ask. I've heard about work camps.

"I've heard about camps," says Krista. "I'm not sure what they do there; they don't show it on TV. Non-Nancys don't have a public image."

"So you never see them?"

"Oh, you see them! I've seen them, shopping and stuff. I feel bad for them."

I feel bad for Krista. It's another new feeling. Sorrow . . . or pity I think. Sympathy? Empathy? It hurts in my eyes.

"Does my mother know about you?"

She looks to Thaddeus for permission.

"He was a girl, you know."

"I know."

"Does that make you afraid of him?" she asks.

"Of Thaddeus? Are you crazy?"

"I am not sure, I may be," she says. I shouldn't say crazy. It's not polite or correct.

"I'm sorry," I apologize.

Thaddeus hangs on the ladder, staring at us.

"Can we be friends?" she asks. "I've never had a friend before."

"Neither have I," I say. "I think we need to tell my mother about you, because you could be of great use to her. But then, yes. Let's be friends."

She hugs me. She will not let me go. Thaddeus, on the ladder, just sitting there, he stares at us, unblinking. His fear changes to anger. His anger changes to sadness. His sadness changes to joy.

"All my girls, together. I will protect you the best I can," he says.

"I will do the same," I promise.

And we climb down the ladder and walk toward the bunker, straight into Francesca's lab.

The walk to the lab is a blur, all metal halls and echo chambers. There are so many handprints on all the metal and glass, the houseboys have not been doing their night-work. I notice Krista is shaking. She is not used to being underground. I give her my sweater. She thanks me.

We walk in, my mom is at her desk, scribbling something. She still uses pen and paper, and then locks it in a safe. Her tech has been hacked many times, and even though technology and security have improved, she is paranoid. It makes sense that she is paranoid—it was only twenty years ago X and his forces rounded up all the women they could in the East and ruined the water supply to the West. They did not drown us like witches, they did not make us thirsty, they left us water in this desert, but it made most—almost all—of the women who drank it infertile. We have well water on the compound. I still drank from outside sources. We're not sure yet if it was enough. My mother might be. She's done my blood work for years. I ask her, she says it's too early to tell. I have never considered until now that she may be lying.

Francesca's office is tacky to me. Only a few people are allowed in it, so she keeps it how she wants. Not the metal and glass and large wood of the rest of the house— her desk is a bright yellow, her chair painted pink. She has pillows and lamps and a little bird in a cage—a red bird, a northern cardinal, that she cloned. The males have the pretty feathers in the species—when I was nine, she was studying them, I asked her why the female ones weren't as pretty, why their songs were not as nice. So she made me a female bird with red feathers and a beautiful song. She said it was just like me. It died a year later, but she keeps making them, always keeping one in her office. Her Avis birds.

She looks up at us and no shock crosses her face. She eyes Krista. She looks at us. It is silent. She motions for us to go on, to talk to her. No one starts. She clears her throat. She looks back down at her papers.

"Mom, this is Krista."

Francesca writes something down.

"Francesca, this is my sister. She escaped from the East," Thad apologizes.

Francesca gets up, locks her notebook in her safe, and turns to us. She takes off her glasses. She puts her hands on her desk.

"Ms. Baron, I can explain . . . " Krista starts.

"Ms. Baron? Please call me Francesca."

"Francesca."

"Krista, do you remember your training? Not what they taught you, but how they did it."

"Some of it. It's coming back."

Francesca puts her hands back on her desk again. She looks up at Krista for a moment.

"You have his eyes."

She walks toward Krista. Thad steps back, I search her hands for weapons. None.

"I am so sorry for what happened to you," Francesca whispers. She holds Krista close. Krista begins to cry. Tears well up in my eyes. I choke them back, no one can notice them. They'll know I'm off my Amplexus.

"I have fought my whole life for you. You've got a family here now," Francesca says. She pulls me into the hug. Thad puts a hand on my shoulder, awkwardly.

Maybe I was wrong about the intuition stuff. Because I wouldn't have expected this in a million years.

CHAPTER 8

Thaddeus

WEST AMERICA IS A FEMINIST Marxist fever dream, and Francesca Baron is their Luminary. She is also the leader of the Scepter, an ancient, secret society. Depending on who you believe, these women may or may not be witches. The Heirs and Assigns of the Scepter have not met in quite some time. They correspond in individual cells, to be certain, but I know, through Francesca, that the entire cohort has not convened in years. They gather now because they feel they must intervene in current events with immediacy and boldness. They have done this in the past: Elizabeth and Mary Queen of Scots is one example. Ellen Bohr and the bomb is another. Eleanor Roosevelt and the New Deal yet another. Throughout history the members of the Scepter have hidden behind men, using them as a mouthpiece. Now they are going to act in the open, as themselves. So this evening is a unique and rare event. I am privileged to witness it. Francesca has allowed me to attend as her secretary, to take notes.

I would enjoy this except for two things: first, the presence of Avis. It's Avis's first meeting, and she is off her Amplexus, and this could be an issue. Second, and more pressing, is the presence of Krista. She arrived from East America, and every move she makes, every utterance, puts me in jeopardy. I have given her a notepad and instructed her not to speak. I have never felt so much like a man from the East. But she is a Nancy. I'm *harboring* a Nancy. It's dangerous. The East could come for her any minute. It is a crime, in this war. She is their property.

I look at Krista, sitting next to me. Francesca gave me specific orders to bring her as an observer, and not let her reveal herself as a Nancy. But—everything she does is strange. She looks way too excited. I made her hide her blonde hair with a cap; I made her dress in clothes that are easy to move in and black—to make her look normal. But still—to me, she does not look normal.

"These women don't have chaperones," she whispers.

"Do not say another word," I hiss.

She draws a smiley face on her notepad and gives me a thumbs-up.

I am screwed. The women of the Scepter are going to sniff her out with ease. It's not a knitting circle or a happy hour club. These women are all united in goals and in heritage. You can't get voted in. You have to be related to an original member and that means knowing and proving your lineage back *thousands* of years. I turn away from Krista and survey the room. There's a slight woman with shaved black hair, a roly-poly woman. I wonder who they are related to. They look as far from Nancys as it is possible to be. Francesca taps the table. The women in the room fall silent. Krista starts to applaud but I smack her hands apart just in time. Francesca notices and smiles at me. She doesn't mean it.

"Thank you all for making the trip here to my home. This is the beginning of a new day. Going forth, we will make our decisions and act in our own names. We will spill blood in our own names, no longer in the names of our husbands. In our own names, we will write the future. Not only for West America, but for the world."

The members nod and murmur in agreement.

"We will begin with our namings. Mears, you may go first."

Mears has short white hair and the face of a beautiful alien.

"I am a direct descendent and scepter of Boudicca, a Celtic queen. Men had a hand in burning down Rome, but Boudicca stopped them. Nero fiddled through the flames, but Boudicca torched the ground Rome stood on. The Romans raped her daughters. They pillaged her kingdom. So she slaughtered them: eighty thousand men, with no mercy."

I write all of this down as quickly as possible.

"After Rome was dead," Mears continues, "Boudicca slit her own throat in the square. Queen Victoria is her namesake; whose Scepter joins us in this room."

I look up in time to see the short, powerful woman stand. As Mears sits the women in the room chant, "May you carry her light and her genes."

I glance at Krista. Her smile is twitching like a machine on overload.

The short woman speaks. "I am the Scepter of Isabella, She-Wolf of France. She accepted her husband's homosexuality, even befriended his lover. But when she took a lover of her own, her husband the king brought her great dishonor. So she gathered an army, captured her enemies, dragged them by horse, disemboweled them, hung them, and then decapitated them and adorned London Bridge with their heads."

"May you carry her light and her genes," I hear. Krista joins in.

Roly-poly offers a curt nod and sits down.

A tall, dark woman with dreadlocks stands. "I am the Scepter of Rani Lakshmi Bai, the most dangerous of India's rebel leaders, who slaughtered her enemies with her toddler on her back."

"May you carry her light and her genes."

A friendly-looking, bookish woman rises. "I am Bella Goldberg. I am the Scepter of Emma Goldman, Jew, free-thinker, and rebel woman, who handed out birth control in the streets, who challenged the thinking of all around her, and who always carried a book so she'd have something to read in jail."

A wave of appreciative laughter fills the room.

"May you carry her light and her genes."

I am mesmerized. As each woman stands and declares herself, pride and valor crossing their faces, it occurs to me how rare it is to know that something important is happening while it actually happens. Turning points—last goodbyes, or train rides where you make the biggest decision of your life, so often go unnoticed. I know I'll keep the memory of this evening vivid forever; it will be like the one of me screaming at the tennis courts. Whatever tonight leads to—and the room feels both magical and ominous—I will keep this memory.

A large-breasted woman wearing an ill-fitted leather jacket rises. "I am the Scepter of Joan of Arc, whose heavenly visions led her country to victory at only seventeen."

This surprises me and I actually gasp. I thought Joan of Arc died childless. There are layers and layers of conspiracies here, I realize. There is much more going on here than I am prepared to understand.

"May you carry her light and her genes."

A woman covered in tattoos stands. "I am the Scepter of Tamar of Georgia, the king of kings and queen of queens, who brought her kingdom to the apex of military, cultural, and financial might."

"May you carry her light and her genes."

The last woman to testify is Francesca. Unless she is sleeping in her lab, she has not slept in weeks; there are feelings even Amplexus cannot stop. Over the years I've known her, she has experienced savage attacks and terrible loss. I have held her in the night while she moans. I have cleaned up glass she has broken in rage, and talked her out of some very unsettling ideas. Now, before this gathering, she stands regally. All women have their own beauty in the West, but true strength stands in a category all its own, and Francesca possesses a beauty that succeeds well beyond the most well-constructed Nancy. Krista is a housecat. Francesca is a jaguar. She clears her throat.

"I am the Scepter of Mary, Queen of Scots, and her cousin, Elizabeth I. In their lifetimes, a great accomplishment for a woman was 'not having features marked by smallpox.'"

There are murmurs throughout the room.

Francesca continues. "The throne was owned by producing heirs, and because of this, a nine-month-old baby was more threatening than an army of men. Mary stood over six feet tall—a height that was considered masculine. She danced and she dressed in ways that were condemned. Most offensive of all: she was both uncommonly beautiful and exceptionally clever."

I glance at my sister. Krista is spellbound.

"History says that Mary died at the chopping block at the behest of Elizabeth. That, in a tragic failure on the part of the executioner, her wig fell into the crowd and her dog refused to leave her underskirts. There is truth in every lie. Her dog was loyal, even if the men around her were not."

There is much agreement voiced throughout the room.

"Men wrote what they consider to be accurate history," Francesca concludes. "Yet women have always been too complex for them to decipher and chronicle."

Cheers fill the room.

"The Scepter is the light of the true and bright," Francesca says, and the women chant: "May you carry her light and her genes."

Then they settle down and wait for the evening's agenda to be revealed.

She's a genius, I think, and not for the first time. There's a way to lead a room full of leaders. If it were my job, I'm sure I'd end up shouting "I'm in charge, bitches!" No one would follow me.

"Who is your mother? What makes you so special that Francesca allows your presence?"

I am startled to find the woman called Mears addressing me.

"My mother is Rosemary Gray of Newark, New Jersey," I say. "Like Boudicca, men took the light from her daughter. Like Isabella, her husband caused her dishonor. Like Rani, she faced a dying country with me on her back. Like Joan, she listened to the voices in her heart, and like Mary . . . " I feel that Krista is about to speak and I take her arm in a vise grip, while saying, "she had a damn convincing wig."

Mears eyes me up and down. She looks hard at Krista. Then she says, "May you carry her light and her genes."

Francesca begins speaking and Mears, mercifully, turns her attention away from me and my sister.

"We've all played a reticent and careful game with our adversaries up until this point." Francesca pauses. "As you well know, I have recently been named Luminary of West America."

There are murmurs of agreement.

"I know that some openly protested this decision."

More murmurs. Krista writes me a note: *I did not know this!*

"These dissenters all have one thing in common: they are men. Ruth, will you please bring them in."

There are expressions of surprise in the room.

A large, square woman enters from a side door. Two men I have never seen before are dragged in. They are handcuffed, and appear to be bewildered, and dazed. Krista writes: *the tall one is handsome!* I take her pad away.

Avis takes my hand. This will not be easy for her.

"It has been said that it is only fair to have male voices in West America. That minorities must be represented," Francesca says. She looks out over her audience. "Yet I have never heard the voice of a single woman in the East American States included in political discourse."

The room agrees; heads nod, seatmates exchange glances.

"We do not want to emulate our enemies. But the men of the East certainly have power. I think it is time we send them a message." She presses a button on her wrist.

"Record. Full room view." We won't be the only ones seeing this. I am glad. Recorded history is the kind we're making now.

At this instant, Ruth reveals an instrument I have never seen before: a small, metal rod. Curved, beautiful, I think it must be some piece to a musical instrument. Or possibly an antenna of some sort. As the room watches in silence, Ruth touches one man with the instrument, then, the other. She caresses their faces in a slow, sexual manner. Then she taps the device with her other hand and the room begins to buzz a bit. Quickly, the sound grows so loud I have to cover my ears. The women sit as before; they are unfazed by the high-pitched whining that now invades my every orifice.

One of the men—the handsome one, he looks at me. Suddenly, I recognize the eyes of a former senator. I recall his name, and realize his daughter used to play with Avis in our backyard. He releases a low wail. As we all watch, his tongue falls out of his mouth. His eyes droop and bulge at the same time. He falls straight to the ground.

The other man tries—and fails—to run. He soaks himself with urine

Ruth touches the second man with her instrument and the buzzing grows louder. The man's hair seems to pop from his body all at once, all of it. As his face withers, his beard falling out onto his shirt, he opens his mouth to whisper something. All that comes out is a fine smattering of blood. And then he, too, is dead.

Many of the women seem shocked; others are delighted. I wonder if I'm going to vomit. I look at Krista; she is stone-faced. She reaches over to my notepad. She writes: *I've seen worse.* ☺

"It's important to send the men of the West a message, and that message is: be loyal to us, or be afraid. Our foremothers dealt with torture and discrimination; their lives existed only to punctuate the men around them. We will not accept that. Men's lives will punctuate ours now! They will be our commas and our exclamation points. They will show us helpful attitudes and kind words, or we will end their lives with a swift period."

The women, as one, clap.

Is this what the old times were like? Gruesome executions got applauded? The further forward society moves, the further backward it retreats—or so it seems to me.

Avis's grip on my hand has not loosened. A tear falls down her cheek.

Francesca directly addresses the camera.

"We have seen the pageant, X. We have heard the song of our sisters. We think you have gotten greedy. We think this girl is too young. She may be just one girl, but if you are breaking the Age Laws, why would anyone in your country keep them? You must lead by example and we are holding you accountable. No child brides. We killed these men, traitors to the West, to show you we have and will use force. However, we'd like to start, like many times before, with a conversation. As the new Luminary of West America, I will accept any invitation to discuss these matters along with many others with you."

She turns off the camera.

"Now for a quick change of tone, I would like to announce that Avis Baron is the newest Heir and Assign of the Scepter. Her heirs and assigns have not yet been revealed to her, as it is not yet time. Does anyone have any thoughts?"

"Happy to have you, Avis," Mears purrs.

"Happy to have you," Krista says. I elbow her.

They look at Avis, expectantly. She is obviously supposed to talk. She lets go of my hand. Her own hands tremble.

"Thank you very much for inviting me. I am flattered, but I am going to have to turn down the invitation."

There are audible gasps in the room. The tension builds.

"I do not think we should be killing men in my basement, and I do not think we should be negotiating with President X. I think we should be negotiating with innocent men and bringing X's head home on a platter."

"No man is innocent," a woman spits back at her.

"No woman is either." Avis shrugs.

"Avis, you are far more advanced then I sometimes realize," Francesca says. "To me, you are a little girl. You were raised in a different world than I, and your resilience impresses me and is a testament to West America. I will take your thoughts into consideration, but you cannot deny membership to the Scepter. There are powers bigger than us, here. History."

"I'm sorry, Mom."

"Francesca. You can call me Francesca."

"No—Mom. I can't. I don't want to."

Avis runs out the door.

Francesca looks at me, her eyes narrow. "Is she off her Amplexus?"

It's going to be a long week.

CHAPTER 9

Nancy159

FOR THE FOURTH ROUND OF the competition, we are separated in the residence so we cannot share tips. The losers are taken somewhere else. No one tells me where, but I no longer can reach them in my mind. After that, we are each chosen by one of President X's current wives to be part of a "team." Our task is to cook and present a small hors d'oeuvre and cocktail party for him. I am chosen by Nancy97. Together we have a small staff to oversee, but I am aware that the majority of the work is up to me.

I am quite nervous about this challenge because 97 is mute.

Today, our government believes that the danger of intellectualism attached to reading and writing is less worrisome to the population than a Nancy that cannot help her beloved or her sister-wives in the simplest tasks. As an example: writing a grocery list. That is a must for an East American girl. It's all very progressive. I learned to write when I was very young. I think my mother taught me. I cannot remember it, like I cannot remember most things—that is an important part of our conditioning. Still, the fact remains that most Nancys before model number 100 cannot read or write. That means I will not be able to converse with 97 at all, not even by notebook.

I will have to try charades. I will not risk planning a party without guidance as to what our President X desires. It occurs to me that there is the possibility that her aim is to be the perfect wife by existing in silence, guaranteeing she will never usurp authority over men, which is genius. So before trying charades I will see if I can get her to speak to me.

I have been taken to meet her in one of the many kitchens the White House has. This one is all yellow and orange, decorated in the style of the American 1970s. I wear a green dress and a perfect pink apron with white heels. I'm waiting at the kitchen table for Nancy97. I have a notebook in front of me, for my own usage. 97 comes in. She sits down across from me and takes one of my hands. She puts it to her cheek with a smile.

"97. I want you to know that I am so happy to have you as my teammate. It is very rude to be inquisitive, and I apologize for what I am about to ask. Please know that

I already love you and want to join you in matrimony to President X."

She nods.

"If you cannot talk because of a physical problem, I understand. But I would like your help in planning this soirée, and if you can talk *at all*, I hope you will do so, because it would help me so much. I truly want to win this pageant."

97 leans back in her chair, away from me. She squints. She nods yes.

"You can talk?"

She shakes her head no, then squints again and moves her head from side to side. She puts out her hand and gestures for me to give her mine. I put my hand in hers. She indicates I should cover my eyes. I do.

Immediately, images flood my mind. *A martini. A pink cocktail with a plastic flamingo in it. A pineapple with little skewers of olives. A cheese platter. A ham with toothpicks stuck in its rind, like a porcupine.* My eyes pop open. The images stop. What just happened? Should I be shocked? Or is this only a new part of Hive Mind? An extension of our powers. Powers? We don't have powers. Of our *talents.* "How do you do that?" I ask.

97 nods and shrugs. *You could do it, too.*

"Did you just talk in my head?"

97 giggles with no sound, all breath and teeth.

Try it! She gives me her hand. I think of a food . . . steak. I picture, clear and deliberate, the steak we ate together.

Too much for a cocktail hour.

"No steak then!" I yelp.

Why were you naked?

"What do you mean?"

With the steak. With my husband.

"Are you angry?"

No. But show me.

She reaches into my mind and I show her the memory and how I felt, how I acted. It plays like a tape, in real time. When the bad word comes up, her hand rises to her mouth and her face has lost its life.

I have lived events like that. But I did not have your word to give him. It was your fault, you know. They should never have granted the right to read. Or taken a girl from West America. A learned woman . . .

"Makes a man's dark predilections come to light. But I'm not a learned woman, 97. And I am not Western. I am an East American. I am a Nancy. I gave him what he wanted. Do you blame me for that?"

No. I can't. It is a sad thing.

I feel her sadness. It wells up in me, and we both weep, silently, as one, so alone and so together.

"How could I have been so stupid? If I had felt less . . . I don't want to lose, 97. Will you show me yours? Whatever your memory is?" I plead. I need to learn from her mistakes.

No. If you don't want to lose, we have a party to plan.

So we do. We plan the party. I do the cooking, she sets the table and we pick the music together. I remark that it is the first time I've been allowed to touch an oven without male oversight. "In training, they told us caution must be exercised because 4 and 7, from the first batch of Nancys, stuck their heads in an oven."

34 did that, too.

She assures me that President X does not expect me to read his mind during the party (and we both find this funny, because she's reading mine), so I must only do my best.

He loves pineapple, which I am allergic to, but I decide I will serve it. We blend many tropical fruits that have been grown in a lab in the capital, we bake a pineapple upside-down cake and assemble a pineapple appetizer tree with toothpicks. Then we put together a beautiful shrimp cocktail.

After a harmonious and beautiful preparation with 97, my favorite Nancy, although I am not supposed to have favorites, we are ready to receive our guests.

President X enters first, with the camera crew, 129, 40, 63, and 3. Immediately, the other Nancys look at the spread. They murmur to each other over the presentation and I can feel their approval; I can also feel their hesitance. I do not smile because I do not want to appear proud. That would be counted as a fault.

"My Beloved." I curtsy and greet him as I offer him a piece of ham on a toothpick.

"You have chosen all of his favorites," 3 observes. She speaks sweetly, but I can feel that she is seething and I realize that pairing me with 97 was a strategy. "Did he tell you?" she asks, playfully touching X's arm.

He chuckles. "This is a pageant, of course I did not tell her. She is gifted, this one. She understands the needs of others, a great skill."

All of the Nancys except 97 are feeling rage.

"How are you today, my dear 159? Did you enjoy preparing this feast for me?"

"Yes, I did. Thank you. It was my pleasure." I am having trouble breathing there is so much anger in this room. 97 starts gasping for air; she plays it off as a cough.

"Grab your drinks, ladies. Let's all sit down," X instructs.

They sit.

"I believe that 159 has a great talent. Or a great defect. A gift. Or a curse. She can reach into the Hive Mind in ways you all cannot."

I know I am not special. The suggestion of it is ridiculous. I am ordinary in every way.

Do not tell him you can hear me.

I hear 97 in my head. I know the danger of being singled out, that a Nancy must never be too separate. I would never tell him I could hear her.

"I am ordinary in every way," I say to X. "May I offer you some pineapple?"

"I say it is okay, dear," X says, and I do not feel threatened by his voice. "In this instance, it is okay that you have a talent. You may be useful to this regime."

"Dear, wouldn't you rather pick one with less spunk?"

"Well, 3. I could understand why a peer might question my choice."

She nods and I feel fear spread through the Nancys as X makes an exaggerated show of looking around the room.

"However, there are no peers of mine here. All I can see is a bunch of things that I own."

"My only thought is your happiness."

"And if I want a new, different thing, you should know better than to question my judgment." Without rising, without warning, without a change in his smile, he punches her in the mouth.

The camera man chuckles. "This will be good for ratings," he whispers to another man with a filming device.

3 grabs her napkin and dips it in water. She wipes the blood from her mouth. "Of course. You are right."

There is no moment of silence but no smiles falter. The party goes on.

"You will go on to the next round, 159," X says to me. "There is one trial left. If you succeed, the rest will be . . . disposed of, and we will marry in six days."

Two men are escorting 3 out of the kitchen. She waves goodbye to all of us. We wave back and continue on, laughing and drinking. I hear screams in my head, but I am not sure whether they are 97's or my own.

CHAPTER 10

Thaddeus

"I AM NOT SURE WHAT YOU'RE SAYING," Avis says to me, gripping the railing that leads out of the bunker.

I shush her. I do not want her mother to hear.

I can no longer lie about this. Not with Krista here. Not with things like they are. I have watched every round of the Last Lady Pageant, and my biggest fear has come true—that Nancy159 will win. Losing means death, but winning is far worse. You see, five minutes ago Avis came straight down the stairs, looked me straight in the eye, and asked me why Nancy159 looks so familiar.

"Where do you think you know her from?" I ask her. "Search your heart."

She closes her eyes. "From a long time ago. From before—from before I lived in this house."

"Who does she remind you of?" Ethan asks, scuttling up behind her. That kid is everywhere lately.

"She reminds me of . . ." That's my girl, she's putting it together.

"Was she a neighbor? A classmate?"

I do not give anything away.

"Who does she remind you of, Ethan?"

I turn on my tech. I turn on the latest round. He looks at it for a long time. I have been taking Avis's Amplexus. It has made me brave. It has made me crazy.

"She reminds me of Avis," he says quietly. "She has the same eyes, and says her Rs the same way."

The color rushes out of Avis's face. She sits on the stairs.

"She is—related to me?"

"How long have you lived here, Ethan?" I ask him.

"Since I was five," he says. "My mother died in the attacks."

"Do you remember anyone else?"

"There were lots of people."

"Kids," I say.

Francesca walks down the stairwell. She was listening. She's going to kill me. I do not mean this as a euphemism.

It's not until she gets to the bottom of the stairs and sits down next to Avis that I realize she's been crying. On Amplexus, only physical pain or emotional distress strong enough to cause physical pain can make a woman cry. She puts her arm around Avis. She kisses the top of her head.

"Do you remember a little girl?" she asks, furthering the question to Ethan, but looking at Avis.

Avis's eyes grow large. Ethan looks like he's going to explode.

"Yes! There was another one. Another baby!" Ethan cries.

"Another me," Avis says.

Francesca nods.

Avis looks like she's shutting down like a robot.

"She's my sister," Avis whispers.

"Your twin," Francesca nods. I never thought Francesca would tell Avis this. I thought the secret would live only in our minds.

"Go away," Avis says to her mother.

"Avis—I can tell you the story—"

"This is not a time for stories. I need some time to myself. Please go away."

Ethan and I turn to leave.

"No. Just her."

Francesca turns and straightens her tunic. She kisses Avis on the head and walks up the stairs.

"I want my privacy, please turn off the cameras."

"Cameras off," Francesca says, for the first time I have known her. The whirring we always hear stops. Francesca walks up the stairs and closes the big, heavy door behind her. She is outside. She so rarely goes outside.

Avis turns to me.

"I'm trained in combat. I have money. I can pay the border guard to get past the wall and into Old Arizona," Avis says to me.

"Where do you think you are going?" I say. "To a summer camp? A water park?"

"There hasn't been a water park in operation for forty-six years," she shoots back, always a literalist.

"If she's my sister I have to rescue her, Thaddeus!"

"Avis . . . there are things I want to tell you . . . ."

"We could take the hovercraft."

I'm surprised she has suggested such a large transgression. The hovercraft is a Todux model—it looks like spaceships from old television shows. Francesca bought it even though it is illegal to fly a hovercraft in West America. So we drive it. Even though you can *feel* the thing wants to fly. Whenever I'm inside it my hands itch with the desire to press the right buttons and have the thing soar into the sky. I told this to Francesca once. She said some things never change. It's ironic to me that a West American company spent so much time and money creating a spaceship, when our country looks like a tumbleweed farm. I guess it fits, though. War destroyed our land, but not its inventive spirit.

"And once we fly into East American territory, what then?" I ask. "You're the very recognizable daughter of a Luminary. You can't simply walk around enemy territory. You can't walk into the White House. What's your plan? And by the way, I know you're not taking your Amplexus."

The silence that follows is a long one.

"You don't understand what you're up against," I say. "Your sister is winning the Last Lady Pageant. This means that she has most likely been successfully brainwashed. And that means she's not your sister anymore. She's someone else entirely."

Avis turns red with anger, with defiance.

Krista says, "There's a chance, though, that her programming's not working. That they stopped her training too early." I notice that her roots are growing out. Still, she's in all her Nancy glory. She's been talking in her sleep lately, and she doesn't wake up right away.

Ethan says, "That's what it looked like on the tech. When she led the singing."

Avis says, "What I know *for certain* is she doesn't deserve to be raped by President X."

"Who said anything about rape?" asks Krista, startled.

"A woman with no agency can't have sex," Avis replies.

"What do you mean by that? What if she wants to?" asks Krista.

Avis stares at her, then at me. "Krista," she says, "my sister doesn't have control over her own mind. How can she consent to sex?"

"Ethan, what we're discussing is very dangerous," I say, breaking the awkward moment. "Why are you involved?" I ask this, even though I'm sure I know the answer.

Ethan's brown eyes lock into mine; they soften. "Thad. For the first time ever, I feel like I have a purpose. I feel alive."

"You know that you could die if you go to East America?"

"I'd rather die than be a houseboy. We're no more free than the Nancys."

The kid's overdramatic. But he has a point.

"So what's the plan?" Avis looks to me for answers.

"We go. We go, we look the part, and we act like we belong there. It's gotten me through the rest of my life. I doubt it will fail me now. But I think we should take Francesca."

"Absolutely not!" Avis barks. "She is the most recognizable person in the West. Our country needs her to survive. It will go on without us. It can't go on without Francesca."

"You don't know who you are, Avis," I let her know, gently.

"I know exactly who I am," she growls. "And I know exactly who my mother is. She betrayed me. To keep a secret like that—she would rather my sister die. She would not allow this. Think of the optics."

She's right, in part. We can't take Francesca.

"The Nancys are a great tragedy," Avis says. "An evil man is a great tragedy. But an even bigger tragedy is us, on the West, ignoring it, lacking the courage to do good. The history books will not remember us well, no matter what we are doing over here. It is our duty. She is my sister."

We will most likely fail. Even though their tech is better than ours, their border surveillance is far superior. I don't really know how to do it and I don't have enough time to learn. But Avis, her mother's child, is right. And it's the best plan we've got.

CHAPTER 11

Nancy159

WE'VE JUST LEARNED THAT THE final round of the Last Lady Pageant is called the Sharing.

I do not know what this means.

I received my invitation this morning in my residence. I arrived at the White House at noon on the dot. My dress is pink and my blush matches it. 97 helped me pick it out. Now, when I step into the Oval Office, the first thing I notice is that the film crew is absent.

"Hello, 159. Glad to see you, please sit down." X gestures to a blue love seat in the center of the room. I sit down. He sits next to me. He looks . . . nervous?

"Men, as you well know, are quite superior to women. What you do not know is that we have our weaknesses."

He pauses to check my reaction. I keep my face expressionless as it hits me. *He's imperfect. An imperfect President X.*

"Our emotional needs," he continues. "These, like our sexual needs, are only catered to by our wives."

I take his hand to show him comfort. His body language has shifted; as I look into his eyes, I see a child. I am confused by this, but I recognize the clue: it is my duty to be maternal in this moment. I put a hand on his shoulder.

"It's unpleasant for me to talk about my past. So I am going to use a technology that plays memories. I want to show you what made me the man I am. Will you watch?"

"Of course I will." I can't believe he asked me. He presses his arm with his finger and a screen appears in the air in front of us. I gasp. Then I giggle.

He is pleased. "You have never seen this technology before. I will tell you a secret: we stole it from the West."

He is pleased with this statement, and he smiles broadly. I never realized how nice his teeth are. He takes my hand and puts it to his face.

"I want you to see me, and love me, for who I really am."

He gently touches his hair, and when he takes his hand away, part of his hair is *in his hand.* It is not real. I do not react. I would never show anyone the way I look without my makeup—thankfully, most of it is tattooed on my face. His display of vulnerability and baldness is very puzzling to me. Is it some sort of trick?

He looks to the screen. My gaze follows his; he takes my hand. On the screen, a little boy appears. The boy is young, poor, and in a place I do not recognize. He is dressed in rags and looks very scared. He hugs a little dog in his arms. The dog and the boy are both very skinny.

"Is that you?" I whisper.

He nods his head yes. He presses his arm with his finger and the vantage point on the screen switches. A woman appears. She is very beautiful; she looks like a Nancy. Older, more tired, but I recognize the bone structure, as well as the color of her eyes and her hair. I turn to him to ask if she is his biological mother, but he gestures for me to keep watching. I notice a bottle of alcohol on the coffee table in front of her, as well as a bottle of pills.

"Mommy?" the little boy says. "Mommy. I'm hungry."

She ignores him. From her right, she picks up a laundry basket and begins to fold some towels. The little boy puts down his dog and runs over to grab a towel.

"What the hell are you doing?" she shouts, looking as if she has just realized he's there.

"I'm helping," he replies, fear in his voice. He folds the towel. His hands are small; he's only four or five, and he does the best he can folding a very large towel.

"That's a woman's job," his mother says, too sweetly now. "Why would you want to do a woman's job? Are you a little girl? Maybe we should dress you up as a girl and call you Stacy."

"No, mommy. I'm a boy." His eyes well up with tears. "I want to help you."

She grabs the towel from him and laughs. He laughs with her and without warning, she whips him in the face with it. "You're a pretty little girl. But you're stupid, and useless, and I wish you'd never been born. Don't you? Don't you wish you'd never been born? Maybe you should kill yourself so I don't have to worry about you. Go where I can't see your disgusting face. Don't come out until tomorrow."

The boy runs away from her; he tries to go out the front door. She grabs the back of his shirt. Urine drips down his leg onto the floor. She picks him up. He looks hopeful for a moment, like he might get a hug. She looks into his eyes. I hope for a happy ending. But she throws him into a closet and then locks the door. You can hear the boy screaming.

The screen goes blank. I look to X. He breathes deeply, to calm himself. I comfort him with a warm embrace. "It's okay. That was a long time ago. It's over now. No one can hurt you."

He sobs into my shoulder. "People can hurt me. Women can hurt me. They can laugh at me and make fun of me, and the women," he takes a big gulp of air, "the women that are not even people, those beasts in West America talk about me like my mother did. I made sure none of them could be mothers. None of them can treat their little boys like I was treated. I did it to make certain no new ones like those animals could be created. Do you understand? Do you understand why I had to do that? Why I've had to do what I did?"

And I do. In this moment, I do understand.

X pauses; his demeanor changes. He slaps his legs with both hands like an excited child. "Now I'm going to show you something else."

It's a talk show. I've seen these and I've seen this one in particular before, in the lobby of my residence. They play things that they find appropriate, and we all watch together. It's enjoyable, because our emotions are enhanced by each other. Watching a ghost movie with other Nancys, for example, is scary beyond what you can imagine. The show is called *Talkin' with Azaria*. I've heard it was recently cancelled. Most of the episodes I've seen attempted to bring West and East Americans on the same stage to talk with one another. In this episode, a woman and an uncomfortable-looking girl sit next to each other. The woman is beautiful in a way I have never seen. She wears simple, black clothes. She has dark hair, and finely arched eyebrows. The girl is dressed like the older woman, which makes me think that woman is her mother, but her skin is far darker, as are her eyes. She looks like she'd rather be anywhere else. Her hair is coarse and unruly; in short, she is everything a Nancy is not. Sitting on the stage with them, Azaria wears a green pantsuit. It looks awful on him in the pink stage lighting. He is what we call a "feminine presence." The West is not as simple as the East when it comes to gender. X huffs in disapproval at Azaria. I've always liked him, but I've always kept that to myself. He has a dark brown complexion, common in the West, and his hair is cut in a high, square shape. As the audience applause dies down, he smiles warmly at his guests. I can't help but smile back.

"Welcome. We're here today with scientist Francesca Baron and her delightful daughter. How old are you, little lady?"

The girl scowls, looking the opposite of delightful, as he says this.

"She is eleven years old," says Francesca.

"As you all know, Francesca is an award-winning scientist and a political activist in West America." He turns to face her directly. "Francesca, I hear you've been very busy," he says. He seems more cautious in this interview than others I have seen him do.

"I have, Azaria," she answers. This woman has a voice like a man! It's higher—but deep, powerful, and vibrant!

I gasp and giggle and look to X. He nods.

"I've spent the last five years in the lab. I'm proud to announce that the next generation of Amplexus is ready to be introduced to the public," she says, authoritatively. Then she pauses, as if waiting for applause. Of course, she's disappointed. The show is filmed in East America.

"I know you had some trouble with the first release," Azaria says, filling the silence.

"We've all had troubles. It's been a very trying time," she says, dismissing his concern. "I'm focused on the future, not the past. It is import to understand that thousands of everyday women have benefited from Amplexus, when taken as prescribed. And now this next generation will enable—"

"It's a very serious drug," Azaria says, carefully. "The side effects can be—"

"Not anymore." The woman waves her hand, as if to erase any complaints. "Amplexus C has all the benefits and none of the side effects. It controls the Weaker Emotions, and has some additional benefits. Women will be at their ideal weights, gain muscle, never tire, and become their best selves. And that's what *you* want in the East, right? It's what we want at Baron Corp. We want women to be their best selves."

The girl next to her picks at a scab on her arm. The camera zooms in on it.

Francesca smiles, broad and toothy. "The new Amplexus is so safe that my daughter, Avis, will begin her first round next week!" she exclaims.

The audience gasps. I gasp, too. I think. I feel woozy. *Avis.* I close my eyes. *Avis. Avis.* I open them. I keep watching.

"Isn't she a little young for that?" Azaria's talk-show personality drops; he seems genuinely concerned.

"You're never too young to be your best self. My daughter has been taking it since she was nine years old." She looks over her shoulder at her daughter. "Right, Avis?"

Avis opens her mouth. She closes it.

Her mother is embarrassed. "Amplexus has what I call the 'Cs,'" she says, quickly. "Calmness, clarity, and the collective strength of women. It might also help with a fourth C, conception."

The crowd reacts immediately. I hear cheers, boos, and audible exclamations of "*What?*"

I can feel the anger radiating off of X. He hates this woman.

"It's important to plan for our future generations, and to amplify what they can do for our cause. It is my responsibility to provide a whole new generation of women with the means to feel the very best about themselves. They will have unfettered access to the Higher Emotions with nothing to temper them."

Azaria is shaking his head, and this irritates his guest.

"Many politicians do not practice their politics at home, Azaria. To them it is a game, and they say what you want to hear when they want to win your votes. I am not such a politician. I am not a person who will say I share your beliefs, and then send your daughters and sons into battle, while keeping my own at home. I believe in what I say and what I do wholeheartedly. I believe in my cause so deeply, that I will make any personal sacrifice for the women of this world. And when I say this, I am speaking for the women in both Americas."

Images of the former U.S., before the Separations, flash on the screen behind the stage in rapid succession. Azaria's face tells me he has no clue what to say and that he hopes she will stop talking.

"Once the dollar collapsed," she says, showing no signs of stopping, "there were a lot of things taken away from us. But we'd been attacked before, and we always rose to the occasion. It was a time when political rivals could have joined hands, men and women both, and forged on. We could have created a country based on equality, liberty, life, happiness."

Images of what I assume is West America flash on the screen. It is a picture of decay. Dusty. Poor. Sad.

"But white men in the former U.S. were privileged. They had a sense of entitlement so ingrained most claimed it didn't exist, that is how much a part of them it was. It started with medical issues. Issues that should have been debated in the open. In a country that was falling so rapidly from worldly favor, they focused on ownership of women's bodies."

Azaria says, "I wouldn't frame it that—"

Francesca Baron cuts him off. "Then, the divorce and marriage laws changed. It started slowly, almost imperceptibly. But one day in the East, women became legal property, thanks to the fascist regime—"

The audience boos and hisses, but Francesca shouts over them. "In a day when the dollar cannot buy you anything women are the new legal tender!"

Nancys appear on the screen. Blonde, identical. I am sure the footage is manipulated. It shows blank eyes and forced smiles. It does not reflect our freedom from choice.

"A slippery slope argument is typically a logical fallacy. Just because things get bad does not mean they will continue to get infinitely worse. Yet this is what has happened. Our nation has been divided . . . our nation was once the greatest country that ever existed! And of the many things President X has stolen from women in the East, robbing a woman of her identity is the most evil."

A few people in the crowd clap. Azaria looks at them, shocked. They stop.

"Azaria, things have to change," Avis says, speaking for the first time. "The Nancys are our problem. All of ours. Even in the West. They are our sisters. It is my mother's duty to *save* them."

Her voice startles me. "Is that . . . was that me?"

"No. That ugly female is your sister. I decided to show her to you. It's part of the Sharing. You get to remember some of your past," X says.

I feel like all the ideas I've ever had of my Self are leaking out of me. I try to think of the words for the thing I'm sitting on, for the room I am in. I've forgotten all of them. "Twins?" I manage.

X looks surprised. He stops the show. "Yes. Twins. You are able to remember?"

I shrug my shoulders. *Maybe the way I can talk to 97*, I think to myself. *Maybe it's because I'm a twin?* I point at the frozen image of Francesca. "Is that my mother?"

"No."

"Who is?" I wonder aloud, not expecting him to answer.

"I don't know," he says.

"Who's my father?"

"You don't have one."

"That girl, she is my twin? Will I meet her? Could she even come to the East? Sorry, I'm thinking out loud."

"You are poorly programmed, that's for sure." He wipes his hand over his bald head. "159. She takes the pill they speak of. Has been taking it her whole life. It changes them. She's not your sister anymore. She's someone else."

I became someone else, too. I became someone else so I could marry you. Or someone like you. I am itchy and hot and my thoughts race in a way I have never experienced. "I need to go to the ladies room," I tell X.

"No you don't. What are you thinking right now? Say it," he demands.

I stop dead in my tracks and stare him straight in his round, old face. "I don't think I am ready to marry."

"You've been able to reproduce for four years," President X reminds me. "But you don't want to marry me? I'll see what I can do. Let's go outside."

He takes my arm in a vise grip and marches me out to the rose garden. X walks me to the podium. The camera crew is here. It's a press conference, a reception, a party, an execution, I don't know. I stand behind him at the podium and a million lights from a million cameras shine in my eyes.

"The Last Lady Pageant is coming to a close," X says into the microphone.

I hear his Nancys laugh, but I'm unsure what the joke is. "It's time for me to announce my decision. Nancy159 and I had a long conversation just now, away from the cameras. We exchanged wishes and desires and our connection deepened. I want to respect her wishes."

I sigh with relief as he takes my hand.

"Nancy159 will be my last wife. The wedding is in six days."

The crowd cheers. He kisses my cheek as tears stream down my cheeks. No one knows what they mean, and no one would care if they did.

CHAPTER 12

Avis

"IS THIS GOING TO HURT?" I ask. I am in Krista's room—in the bunker, of course. Francesca has not yet returned. It has been nine hours. The cameras in the bunker are still off.

Krista laughs. "No. I'm not going to do to you what they did to me. What they did to me was surgical. I was put in a coma for three days and then sedated for another three weeks."

"That sounds horrible."

"It was! And then I had a tiny painkiller problem . . . but that's neither here nor there. First thing's first, let me put on some music and put out some food."

Krista puts out a plate of pink mini-cupcakes and puts on some music.

"What is this?" I inquire. I've never heard anything like it before.

"It's surf rock," she says, like I'm simple. "My old Beloved used to love it. Sit down."

I sit down at her vanity. She took so many suitcases from the East—I only own eleven items of clothing. They are all high quality—but still—that's all you need—at least it's all you need in the West. Her suitcases have bold, floral patterns on them. She has a large pink case filled with makeup of every kind, even prosthetics! I thought Nancys didn't know anything, but I was wrong. She spins the chair away from the mirror and looks me in the eye. "No peeking!" She goes to work on me, and whatever she's doing, it sure hurts my eyebrows.

"So," Krista's voice gets the pink tinge of gossip. "Have you had sex with Ethan yet?"

"No!" I exclaim. "In the West, it's different," I explain. "We don't have sex."

"You don't have sex? Before marriage, you mean?"

"There's no marriage. That's an old, misogynist tradition. It involved giving women away. Like they were goats. The whole thing was meant to celebrate virginity."

"But you don't have sex?"

"Nope."

"How does the West stay populated?"

"Science. You don't need men to have a baby. You don't need people, even."

"That sure sounds like virginity's important here in the West. More important than it is in the East, I can assure you." She winks at me.

"Purity isn't important," I clarify. "But protecting yourself from sexual violence is. And honestly, when you give yourself over to a man, all acts of sex are sexual violence. That's what Francesca teaches."

"Why do you call your mother that, Francesca?"

I shrug. I don't know. "I've always called her that."

"I think of sex like a job. Or going to the doctor. It's something that's done to you, not something that you do. It makes someone else happy." Krista laughs. "I guess you don't go to the doctor to make him happy, though."

Thad walks into the room. "I'm sorry. I couldn't let you two continue this conversation. I'm a man, but I was a woman, physically. I've had sex. As both. And everyone is just wrong on both sides."

Krista stops what she is doing. "Enlighten us, then," I say.

He sits down on the bed. She starts pounding white powder on me. It burns a little. It feels like bugs on my skin.

"Krista, love is not enduring cruelty. That's abuse. And Avis . . . it's complicated out there in the world. The old patriarchy didn't want boys to claim their feelings, and they wanted women to deny them. So when West America was built, the ideal of women not having sex . . . it was for political reasons, powerful ones," Thad orates.

"You're so smart," Krista gasps. "How did you get so smart?"

"You're smart too, Krista. You've just forgotten," he assures her.

"Am I not smart?" I ask.

He doesn't answer; instead he says: "I'm not simply sharing my opinions. I read a great deal and I'm sharing the wisdom of the great thinkers of before our time. Audre Lorde. bell hooks. Before the war, there were people—women, mostly, who understood these things. They knew that love can rescue and redeem. They were great women, and we didn't listen to them. They could have saved us all. Avis, the reason it's dangerous to love Ethan . . ."

I start to object but he keeps speaking—"the real reason sex would be dangerous, is that you could both be killed. But not because sex itself is violence. It's because the government in the West doesn't want you to form loyalties to a man. In the past, that wasn't entirely crazy, and it was based in fear. But times have changed."

"My mother hasn't."

The silence is horrible.

Krista says, "You're looking great, Avis." She is smearing something all over my arms to lighten my skin.

"Let me help," Thad says. "I always did Mom's wigs."

Suddenly, a dead blonde animal starts its new life pinned to my head.

"I missed you," Krista says to Thad. Thad has tears in his eyes.

I'm surprised. "Did you remember Thad while you were there? With your husband?" I ask.

"I dreamt of him; they control many things, but never our dreams. And then I . . . read something and I remembered things I had forgot and forgot things I remembered."

I take a deep breath. I'm ready to ask the question I've been avoiding. This fear feeling is for real. "What, exactly, do you think President X is going to do to my sister?"

"They portray him as kind to his wives," says Krista.

"Kind how?"

"Kind . . . in the way a show dog owner is nice to his show dogs. But since my Waking, I don't know anymore what's real and what isn't."

She hands me a floral dress, white pantyhose, something that goes around your waist and looks painful, heels, and a bra that appears to have large breasts sewn into it. She points to the bathroom as I strip and put it on.

"They're not modest here," Thad explains.

I put all the crazy accoutrements on; Krista helps me hook the bra. "Can I see now?"

I look in the mirror. I touch my face. This cannot be me. My brown skin is painted white. The wig is chin-length, blonde, and curly. My brown eyes are framed in dark lashes. I look like . . . well, like a Nancy. "Beauty in the East is pretending to look like someone else," I say.

"It isn't an idea that started in the East! In the old USA actresses would make up a persona," Krista explains.

"They would change their voices, their hair, their nose, their breasts, until they looked like an image in their heads. Or a person who lived a long time ago."

"Why? I don't always like the way I look, but at least I know who I am."

"Authenticity isn't a value everyone shares," Thad explains to me softly.

"My sister shouldn't have to do this," I say. A tear slips down my cheek. Krista dabs it so I don't ruin my makeup.

"Many of your sister's changes are permanent," Thad says.

"Did Francesca give her away?" I ask.

"I can't explain all that to you," Thad whispers. "It's not my place."

"Do you know her name at least?"

Thad leans toward me. He whispers in my ear, "It's Nyx."

Nyx. I remember that name! My sister's name is Nyx.

"When was the last time I saw her?" I ask.

"At about three, I think," Thad answers. "No more questions, we have to get moving."

I strike a power pose, hands on hips.

"Heroes come in all forms," Krista says, sounding amazed.

Thad picks up an outfit that looks like it's from an old movie on the bed—short pants, a coat with tails, etc. Something straight out of *Pinocchio*.

"Oh my Goddess, is this for . . . " Thad trails off.

"It's for Ethan," Krista laughs.

I laugh too. It feels good to laugh. It's been a while. It'll probably be a while longer.

We're going to East America.

CHAPTER 13

Nancy159

MY WEDDING IS IN SIX HOURS.

After the announcement I felt despair. My body turned to a different substance. It was like lead. Or another heavy metal. I don't know the names of any others. Only lead. I asked 97 what I was feeling in my mind. *Despair*, she told me. *It is the complete loss or absence of hope.*

I don't know what to do next. Today is my wedding, I've won the pageant and I'm going to have the wedding I've dreamed of since I was a little girl, and yet I'm here hoping a comet will hit the earth in the next hour or so. I try not to let it show. I sit with the other wives in the Nice Room for Mean Things. This is my life now. They can all feel my mood.

"You're an ungrateful little bitch," 3 tells me.

Maybe she's right. I can't bother to answer her.

We try to breathe together, several times. They can't snap me out of it. 129 brings out dress after dress. I don't care which one we choose. They are all the same: big, white, gaudy.

I try on a strapless one with a white bow at the middle. It's long, but no train. I feel weighed down enough as it is. Something inside me has shifted. I feel alone for the first time. I am alone in my own head. I am alone on this swiftly tilting planet. I am alone in this life.

I can't hear you anymore. 97 puts the words in my head.

I'm not thinking anything. I look at her. I don't care what these Nancys think of me. It won't change anything. "Don't you ever want to do anything else? Besides this?"

"Your programming is terrible," 63 says.

3 tells me to sit so she can do my makeup. I sit. Now she's hurting me on purpose, but I won't show my pain because she would like that.

"What else would you do?" 3 says, nearly poking my eyeball out with a white eyeliner.

"I'd like to see the ocean," I say. What I don't say is I'd like to get in it and never come out. I close my eyes and let the fantasy wash over me in waves. "I'd also like to meet my sister."

"Your sister is a West American whore," 3 reminds me.

"You have to pick a maid of honor," 129 says.

"97," I say without hesitation. The rest look offended. "It's not like you like me."

"It doesn't matter what we like!" says 3. "It matters what X likes. He is our Beloved. Our reason for being. He is why I will put up with you for the rest of my life."

The rest of my life. The rest of my life. Such a long time. *What happens after?* I wonder. People used to think that they went to heaven, or became an animal. I wouldn't mind being an animal. No one comes after you and takes your mind and spirit. No. I don't want to be an animal. Not gills or feathers or fur. *I want to be a man next time.* I hope God or whoever hears me.

I can hear you, 97 says.

Stop. It'll only make you sad, I tell her.

I get up and walk to the steel-reinforced bathroom. I stare in the mirror. I look beautiful, I guess. Whatever that means. There is a small shower. In the shower is a razor. Our bodies are always to be hairless. They do full-body laser removal as part of our conditioning, but honestly, I'm not sure how well it works. I pick up the razor. The razor is metal and pink. Looking at it, I have a memory. I close my eyes and let it wash over me.

I'm three years old. My sister—my sister!—and I are in the basement of an old building. Some room without windows. I don't know where it is, but we're in a kitchen. Maybe it's our home? Her hair is the color of tangerines. She points under the kitchen sink.

"Sissy, there's a turtle under there. It lives in a pot under the sink. You can't see it. It's mine."

I run out of the room. A dark man—he looks like a woman, somehow—sits in the next room. I ask him about the turtle. "There's definitely a turtle living in there," he says, solemnly.

I am thrilled. I have always wanted a pet.

The man goes back to his book. *Thad.* His name is Thad.

In my real life in my real body, I feel the razor on my wrists.

In my memory, I run back, and without a moment's hesitation, I rip the pot out of my sister's hands. The turtle will be mine! I open the pot. It's full of old spaghetti. She laughs and laughs. I laugh too; but I still throw a handful of spaghetti at her before running to the living room to throw the rest at the dark young man. Who is that man? He pretends like the spaghetti is killing him, he gags and rolls around on the floor as if I've murdered him with a fistful of noodles. Then he hugs me so tight I snort.

I open my eyes and I am on the floor. What a beautiful memory. I lay on the cold floor, blood on my white dress. I think of X for a moment. I wonder if he feels this . . . despair. Even in my dying I think of him. Him, him who I once thought of as my Beloved. Maybe after this, he won't take another wife. I can save one. This is the best and only choice I have. The room greys and for the first time since I can remember, I feel happy and alive.

CHAPTER 14

Ethan

I CAN'T STOP LOOKING AT AVIS. Well, I can never stop looking at Avis, but it's usually for a different reason. After her makeover, she looks—she looks like Krista. I'm not saying Krista looks bad, she doesn't, she looks like Krista. I want Avis to look like Avis. But it's for safety. It's not permanent. I keep telling myself that. Besides, I have bigger problems, like the fact that I'm dressed like Geppetto and I'm probably going to die any minute.

"Everybody hold on," Thad says.

The Todux whirs and bells ring, then we're hovering off the ground. "You can't un-ring a bell," Francesca once growled at me when I burnt some quinoa. You can't un-fly a Todux, either. Though I guess you could just land it, but . . . whatever. My stomach goes into my throat as we take off and whir away. "You're sure we won't get shot at?" I ask everyone.

Thad and Avis look at me with pity in their eyes; Krista looks worried. I wonder if I'll die first. Probably. Thad's been taking Amplexus. I know because it's sticking out of his pocket.

Thad presses a button. I feel tingly all over my entire body.

"As I've told you numerous times, this is a vehicle available in East America so they won't automatically suspect us unless we're searched," Thad says.

"And there's the obscuring technology so we're pretty hard to detect," Avis adds.

I should have clarified this much earlier. "Are you saying we're invisible?"

"Yes," she sighs. "That's exactly what I'm saying."

We whir into the darkness. My first adventure, and it may be my last. I take Avis's hand and squeeze it.

CHAPTER 15

Avis

THE TODUX WHIRS OVER THE WALL that divides our countries, and I feel my hands start to shake. No matter what disguise I'm wearing, I don't believe anyone will be convinced that I'm a woman from the East. Walking in these shoes—if you can call them shoes—is an unexpected difficulty. Francesca once told me that high heels were made to present a woman's rear end for breeding; they make your behind stick out. I'm not sure if that's true, seeing as how I now know her to be a liar. But another thing she said is that they were made so we cannot outrun men.

That, that I believe. I keep on practicing my balance.

"We're here," Thaddeus informs us, as if we aren't fully aware of where we are.

I look out the window. I haven't been here in years. Everything looks different from the West. It's not dusty. It's not dirty. There are no tumbleweeds or wild dogs. It is spic-and-span, perfectly landscaped, and there's not a human being in sight. Rows of perfect, identical houses line the streets. They vary in color a bit, from blues to pinks to yellows, but they are all the same house. I've read about it in history books. But I didn't expect it to feel so barren, so haunted.

Krista points to our northwest. I follow her finger and see a sign that reads VISITOR PARKING in bright, neon letters. I bet you could see it from space. "Are you serious?" It seems like a trick to me.

She looks at me like I'm stupid. "That's where visitors park. There's a lot of parking in the East. We pride ourselves on our well-organized society."

"What about your complete lack of security?" I inquire.

"That's what the wall is for!" She smiles.

"But—you can just dig under it . . . " I reply.

"Or fly over it!" Ethan interjects.

"I'm not parking there. Might as well wear a sign that says 'kill me,' " Thad says.

"We can park in the street," Krista says.

So Thad parks in the street. It's silent. "We're only a few miles from Old D.C.," he assures us. "Remember, be careful who you talk to."

Ethan has turned a pale shade of greyish blue. Krista doesn't seem worried in the slightest, which I appreciate.

We get out of the Todux and leave the obscuring tech on. It would be too big of a risk otherwise.

"Is it weird that there's no one around?" I ask. I walk slowly in my painful shoes.

"No one lives here! This is for show!" Krista laughs. She goes up to a house and knocks on the door. No one answers. Then, she opens the door. Behind it, a brick wall. It is just a façade. The four of us walk onto a tree-lined road. We walk past the perfect, identical houses I saw from the air. I observe that even the rocking chairs on the front porches are the same.

"Government issued," Krista boasts.

"Did you have a house like this?" Ethan asks her.

"Most people don't live like this. This is the capital."

"Are any of these houses real?" I inquire.

"Some," Krista responds flippantly. I sense something in her tone; it is forest green and it might be fear. I realize I am forest green all over. I would ask Thad for an Amplexus, but I know he left them in the car. It's too dead a giveaway.

We walk down a perfect block and turn right onto another perfect block. Thad has his tech out on a very small hologram and is leading us when, unexpectedly, we hear a polite cough behind us.

We turn and see an odd man in a suit. He's a small man with small arms, yet regular-sized hands. Short legs, yet regular-sized feet. He has a bald head, yet a mustache. His proportions are all completely wrong but he is friendly looking, if not harmonious.

"Hello, visitors!" he says, his voice deeper than I'd imagine. "I am Melonius, your tour guide for the East!"

What the hell is this? I wonder.

"We don't need a tour guide," Thaddeus objects, astonished.

"Oh, but you do! We want to make sure you see E.A.'s best! I can tell you two gentlemen are visitors to our lovely city. Are you here on business or pleasure?" I do not trust this man. No one does, by the looks of it.

"Pleasure," Ethan replies.

"How do you know these two lovely ladies?" Melonius asks. Curiosity tinges his voice navy blue around the edges.

"They're our sisters," Thad explains.

Melonius behaves as if Krista and I are not capable of speaking for ourselves. This is how men treat women in the East. I've known this all my life but this is the first time I'm experiencing it. It makes me feel so small and unimportant.

"Wonderful!" Melonius exclaims. "Family is always the most important thing. Follow me. What would you like to see: our women, our food, a tour of the White House?"

"We're here for the wedding," Thad says.

"Ah! So you have invitations?"

We glance at Krista. She said we wouldn't need them!

Melonius senses something is awry. "I will make efforts to obtain some for you. In the meantime, you must be hungry?"

"Food would be great," Thad mumbles.

"Of course! Right this way."

We follow Melonius down the middle of the empty road. We walk about a half mile before I spot an oddity. Daffodils line the streets. I am not a botanist, but daffodils only live a few days; I know this because they are my favorite flower. Yet none of these look dead or wilted. There is also little to no variation in their color. I bend down to look at one.

"Don't inhale that!" Krista shouts, too late.

I cough. The daffodil smells like plastic and spray paint.

Melonius looks straight at me.

"She's such a dumb banana!" Krista giggles. "You know they're not real, Amanda!"

Who is Amanda? Oh, I'm Amanda. Right. I giggle. "Oh my gosh I'm so dumb. They just look so real. I thought these might be different."

Melonius nods. "New models. Glad you like them."

I nod enthusiastically. Chemical residue burns my nose and throat. Ethan touches a leaf on a tree. I look at him quizzically. He nods no and grimaces.

Fake plants. They line their empty streets with fake plastic plants. Why? What purpose does that serve? A decorative one? I cannot comprehend it. Francesca has told me the East still struggles financially—this is what they chose to spend their money on? I lurch along in my horrible shoes.

"Poor Amanda hurt her ankle dancing three days ago," Krista purrs to Melonius.

He gives me a comic pouty face. "How sad."

"Yes. I am so sad." I laugh. Everyone joins in and laughs with me. Ethan's fake laugh is horrible.

The longer we walk, the more amazing it is to me that there is not a piece of trash anywhere. Not a trash can. Not a cigarette butt. Not a piece of litter. Nothing. It really is just for show. There is no way anyone lives here.

We arrive at a pink house just like the others, but larger. It says "Visitor Center" on the front. We follow Melonius's lead, wipe our clean shoes on the welcome mat, and walk inside. I'm surprised to see women inside; they appear to be real women, at least. The East doesn't have the money or tech for this many robots, as far as I know. They are all identical, all Nancys.

"These are some Nancys-in-training. They're taking some time away from the Residence," Melonious boasts as he smacks one on the rear. She giggles and my blood boils. I turn away.

"Sit down, they will serve you."

We sit at a large wooden table, but when I tap the wood, I realize it is synthetic. Plastic made to look like wood. It's like we're in a large dollhouse. The Nancys start bringing us plates. They move almost in unison. The serving is choreographed, like a dance. At first, I assume their unity comes from a terrific amount of practice, but as I watch them, I fear that the explanation is darker than that. This is what programming looks like. It's one thing to read about, or see on the tech. Quite another to witness it.

They bring us Jell-O casserole. Vienna sausage. A loaf of Spam with peas in the center. A large gelatinous mold made out of blue cheese. Colorful food with no nutritive substance. Krista and Ethan chow down right away. I take a few crackers and some strawberries—most likely lab-grown. I try to eat them in a "ladylike" fashion, taking tiny bites.

One of the Nancys—a particularly young one, she looks about thirteen—comes to refill my water. She looks into my eyes as she does it. Her expression is forlorn, as if she's trying to communicate something to me.

"Are you okay?" I ask, quietly.

She freezes, pouring the water. She just keeps pouring. The glass overfills and I jump up and pull my chair out of the way. Water flows onto the table, onto the floor.

Swiftly, Nancys appear from all over the place: ones we haven't seen before. Eight or nine of them, in total. They carry her out of the room. She kicks a little bit; she struggles against them, but it's half-hearted. It looks like she's trying to do synchronized swimming in their arms, toes pointed, graceful limbs.

"Please excuse 467," Melonius says. "She's very new." He takes a bite of gelatin.

Thad nearly spits out his blue cheese gelatin when he hears that number. "I thought there were only a couple hundred," he says, sounding casual. I can see he's trying to stay calm.

"We've greatly enhanced our programming. Today, it's cheaper, and quicker," Melonius informs him. "We plan to have ten thousand by the end of this year. Four years from now, we'd like to give every woman in East America the privilege of being a Nancy. Isn't that exciting, Amanda?" He winks at me. "We want to make our females the happiest. So, cheers to the Nancys!"

He raises his glass. We all follow suit. I grip my glass so hard I think it might break, but luckily, it's plastic, like everything else in this hellscape they call a country.

The meal ends without further catastrophe, but I feel weird and hollow. I look around the table; I don't think I'm alone. Thad, Ethan, and even Krista look shell-shocked.

The Nancys clean up the dishes. They thank us over and over again. I am not sure why they are thanking us: we did nothing. They gave us food and cleaned up after us. They seem to only say "thank you" and "I'm sorry." "I'm sorry" is used for an event like walking near you. "Thank you" is taking away a plate of cracker crumbs. It's more unsettling than I'd imagined it would be.

"Across the street, there's an empty house," Melonius informs us. "The blue one. Since you have no plans and no tickets yet, you folks must stay there for the night. I'll meet you there at eight on the dot to bring you tickets to the wedding."

"Tickets?" Thad asks.

"Yes, I assume you are here for the wedding. We invite any citizens that wish to witness it. I thought more would come. It's not a great year, though, financially. But we are very happy to have you!"

He opens the door to the pink house, ushering us outside.

"Do we need a key?" Ethan asks.

"We don't have keys in West America. No need," says Melonius.

We make our way across the street to the small, blue house.

It looks like picture books from the 1950s. Floral patterns, lace doilies. A museum of a time that repulses me, but that the East reveres. "It was simpler then," X always says. Maybe for him.

***

The bed that Ethan and I share at Little Blue Creepy House is soft, pink, and glorious. We've never been alone this long, and—my Goddess—it is so wonderful. I can't believe Krista and Thaddeus allowed it. This might be my last night on this earth. My defenses are down, and love fills me at a cellular level.

"I love you," we echo, over and over, as we look into each other's eyes. He strokes my arm. I stroke his beautiful, perfect face. Our lips meet. I've never felt longing like this. Our bodies intertwine. It feels dangerous.

"We can't. I could get pregnant," he insists.

"Wouldn't that be wonderful?" I hear myself say. "A new life, made out of the two of us, a miracle."

"But we can't be together; we can't be a couple. We can't be seen together in public."

"Ethan. Let's get married. Let's get married and stay here in East America in this little blue house forever. You are the only thing that matters."

"Yes!" he yells.

"Yes! Yes! Yes!" I yell, for the same and different reasons.

We begin our journey to ecstasy. "I'm going to . . . I'm going to . . . "

"Avis wake up."

I sit up in bed. "Ow!" My head hits something. Oh, it's the ceiling. Oh. I'm not having unprotected sex with my groom-to-be. I'm in a bunk bed in a fascist country above Krista.

"What time is it?" I mumble, groggily.

"It's 6:00 a.m. We have to re-Nancy you."

The last thing I want to do is put on that horrible, horrible makeup. It feels like bugs crawling on my skin. But I get out of bed. I shower. I sit in my ridiculous Nancy underwear while Krista hums some nonsense song. She redoes the whole thing. Slathers on the whiteness. Wig. I thought combat training was bad. This is worse.

By eight o'clock we're ready, in our East American finery—the closets were filled with clothes, on top of the ones that Krista brought. I can't look at Ethan, due to that dream I had in which we did intercourse. And then I offered my hand in marriage, which is not a thing you can do in West America. I am so embarrassed by myself. I wish I had brought my Amplexus.

At 8:03 a.m., a robotic voice proclaims: "A LEARNED WOMAN BRINGS A MAN'S DARKEST PREDILECTIONS TO LIGHT."

"What the hell?" Thad says. He looks weirded out.

It happens again. "ALL HAIL PRESIDENT X."

"It's the doorbell!" Krista explains, all blonde hair and smiles. She opens the door and there he is. Melonius.

He welcomes us all at the front door. We nod and exchange pleasantries. He's brought a small, two-seater golf cart. It's nice to see a vehicle on these empty streets, even a simple one.

"Good news and bad news," Melonius says. "Good news, I got you invited to the wedding! Bad news: I can only bring one of you. I choose Amanda. I'll have her back by midnight. Most definitely, I will have her back."

My stomach goes up to my throat. I'm in fight-or-flight mode. My skin tingles everywhere. Everyone just stares at him, agog.

"Of course," I say. I don't need Amplexus to be brave, I tell myself. "Let me get my . . . purse." I have never said *purse* before.

"She's just a woman," tries Thad. "Surely a man should—"

"It's my decision. It's final," says Melonius. He holds his hand out for me.

"Melonius," I say, sweetly. "Is there any way we could all go? We are all so very excited about this . . . union. It would be a shame for them to miss it, don't you think?"

Melonius extends his arm. "Your chariot awaits, my lady."

I don't know why they worry about me. I'm the martial arts expert. These heels—I can walk in them now. Victory.

He's small. I could take him, I think as I get in the passenger seat. As he drives away, he says, "Did you think I didn't know that was a tranny, Avis Baron?"

I hide my shock. "They don't say tranny in the West. Did you know that?"

"Oh. Then what do you call that thing?"

"We call him a man."

Melonius drives us toward the White House. I see it crumbling in the distance. I realize I'm shaking like a leaf. This man knows who I am. I tell myself that leaving the others might not have been the best choice, but at least I made one. At least I was able to choose.

CHAPTER 16

Nancy159

NO ONE HAS SPOKEN TO ME since I tried to die. I haven't uttered a word, either.

They're watching me. They're watching me all the time. Today is my wedding day.

They made a new dress for me. It has long sleeves, to cover where I slashed my wrists. Nancy3 found me on the floor in the bathroom. She woke me up, then she spat on me. She told me I was weak, a coward.

This is supposed to be the happiest day of my life, when I serve my purpose. How am I supposed to serve my purpose when I don't even know my own, true name? There are so many things I'm unsure of. The only thing that I know for certain is true is *I have a sister.*

So they sewed sleeves on my new dress. This one is lace, the other one was shiny crinoline. I'm in the Nice Room for Mean Things, a vanity is set up. It's my Time Alone. Before a Nancy's wedding, I've been told, she gets her Time Alone. I've been alone for about six minutes; it's the longest I've been alone since I tried my best to die.

I wouldn't let anyone touch my hair, wouldn't even wash it. So they put a wig on me. They won't let me in the bathroom alone. They took me outside and sprayed me with a hose so I wouldn't smell bad. It was cold, but it felt good. Maybe they'll do it again tomorrow.

"Are you still there?" 3 barks as she enters the room.

I'm not surprised to see her. I didn't think they were going to leave me alone for too long. I don't know what they are afraid of: there is no way I could kill myself in here. You can't drown yourself on shag carpet.

3 sits down in front of me. She looks into my eyes. I'm not going to talk unless she makes me.

"I can't see in your mind."

I shrug. She sighs.

"Traditions are very important to us, to our family, which you are joining, whether I like it or not. Whether you like it or not. Each of the wives will come in and give you a piece of advice and a gift. My piece of advice for you, 159, is to give up. Give up the part of yourself that's resisting this."

I'm surprised that she says this.

"You think you're the first? You're not. I know you think you want to die, but if you don't go through with this, he'll kill you. Not personally, but he will have you killed. It will be long. It will hurt. They will torture you."

We stare at each other as her words hang in the air. Tears well up in my eyes.

"Or, you could have the best life of almost anyone in the world," she says. "Isn't that what you truly want?"

"I want to see my sister."

"What is this obsession? *This* is your family! *We* are your sisters! You could have a *child*. You could give us all a child. Your fertility tests look better than most. Why do you think he picked you, for your horrible personality?"

"My fertility tests?" I ask, wiping my nose through my tears.

"Yes! You are a 70 percent chance of being fertile. That's the highest we've seen in quite some time."

I just stare at her. I don't care. She throws up her hands. "I'm going to give you something old. It will help you." She hands me a basket. "Just outlive it, okay?"

She leaves the room. I look at the basket. I don't want to open it. But then, it moves. Then it *squeaks*. What on earth? I slowly open the basket. Inside is an old, small dog. A dog! People rarely have pets these days; radiation from the war made most domestic animals dangerous, and they were put down. The dog is black and small, with dark eyes. To me it looks a little like a monkey. It is not cute. It is old and fuzzy and smells like a can of fish for some reason. It has a pink bow on it. On the bow, "Obedience" is written in a feminine script. I put the dog in my lap. She licks my face.

I can't help it. I love this gift, this dog. This was *nice* of 3. I never thought 3 could be nice.

I decide her name won't be Obedience. I will name her; I will give her a number. Just like I have. But not a number like a Nancy has . . . Maybe not a number, but a measurement. Inch? No. Too scary for a name. Centimeter? No. Too formal . . . Teaspoon. That's it. I will name her Teaspoon.

I hug her and she lets out a tiny squeak. She must weigh about five pounds. Food is all around the room. What do dogs eat? I put a large platter of cheese on the floor, then I rethink it. I give her a piece of synthetic meat. I lay on the floor and watch Teaspoon. I love her.

40 enters the room. "Get off the floor," she demands.

I don't respond so she picks me up and puts me in a chair.

"That dog is ugly. 3 is too kind to you."

"Her name is Teaspoon," I say. I wish Teaspoon would growl at 40. She doesn't even look up. Teaspoon is not going to protect me.

She regards me warily. "My advice is basic. They used to say, do not go to bed angry. But that's hard. So my advice is: Don't keep score. Don't have expectations. Disappointment makes him angry. If you keep expectations at bay, you'll get punished less."

I nod.

"My gift is something new. Since you've never been kissed, I am going to kiss you. You will know how to kiss before your wedding night. I don't want you to be embarrassed."

I should object to this, but realize that X didn't treat her like he treated me. This will be the first real kiss I've ever had, and I welcome it. She leans into me. She smells like cookies. Her lips touch mine. They kiss mine. I stay still.

"Kiss me back," she demands. She kisses me again. I pucker. She really does smell good.

"That's not going to please him. But that's not my problem."

40 starts to walk out. I take her arm. I pull her back to me. And I kiss her like we're the only people on earth. Time stops. I kiss her and kiss her and kiss her and our tongues touch. I'm breathing hard.

She breaks it off. "Have a happy wedding day."

She leaves the room. "Did you see that, Teaspoon?" Teaspoon's still trying to eat the same piece of meat.

97 and 63 come in together; since 97's mute, she doesn't get to see me alone. I'm disappointed. Expectations are bad though, I remind myself. 97 points to the dog with excitement. She immediately takes the piece of food, pulls it into three pieces, and feeds her a piece one by one.

63 says, "My advice is keep up your figure. It gets harder as you get older. Watch the sweets."

I thank her. "Also, here's my gift. It's borrowed. You can borrow it from me."

She gives me a hair comb made of pearl. It looks very old. It must be an heirloom, given to her by someone important.

"It was the first Nancy's. Her given name was Nancy. She is part of all of us. And now you are, too. Please do not kill yourself. You're our best hope for a baby around here."

"Can I have a moment with 97?" I ask.

"I don't care." And 63's gone.

97 looks down at her dress. She is in her bridesmaid's gown. It's red and white stripes at the bottom, floor-length. Blue at the top. East America kept the USA's colors. *It's awful.*

I know. I want to give you something borrowed, as well. Your wedding night, I will be sleeping in the room next door. I have arranged it. If it gets too much, if you want me to, I will enter your mind, and I will be there for you. Not with you, for you. I can take over. You'll still have to watch. But I'll keep your eyes closed as best I can.

"Do you have any advice?" I ask her.

A tear runs down her face. *Please, try to live. My life is much better with you.*

I hug her as hard as I can. Teaspoon sees this and jumps around our ankles. We laugh. After a moment, 97 leaves too.

Then 129 comes in. "Hi 159! I love that we share 9 in our names. It's really special."

She's doing the thing where you pretend everything is great and nothing is wrong.

"How old are you?" I ask. I realize I've never thought to ask her.

"Sixteen."

She's the same age as me. She must have been—

"It was my thirteenth birthday."

I nod. I don't say anything. I don't want to make things worse for her.

"I had my period, I wasn't a little girl. Don't worry. As for advice . . . there's an old man in the basement named George who's super nice and will cook for you anytime you want. He's very kind and asks nothing of you. He'll also give cooking lessons. I'll go with you if you want."

"I'd really like that," I lie.

She starts to leave. "Oh! Your present! I forgot. Something blue. Well, these are borrowed, too. Don't tell anyone." She hands me a large bag of blue pills.

"I call them Nancy's Little Helpers. They get me through rough days. Government issued, totally safe."

I open the bag and take one.

"The other thing is . . . I want to show you, if we can connect. I didn't come to the capital until I was seven, so I saved some memories. This one, well. It's blue."

I close my eyes. She puts her forehead to mine. I see water in front of me, as far as the eye can see. I feel hot sand on my feet. The water goes on forever. The sun sets on the horizon.

"It's the ocean," she whispers.

I've always wanted to see the ocean. I stay with her, in her memory, for quite some time. The air is cold. The sun is bright. The water gleams and glistens with life.

"Thank you," I whisper.

With that, she leaves. I'm not sure if the pills do anything. I feel the same. A few minutes later, a little man with short arms and long hands and a mustache comes and gets me.

"My lady, it's time," he says.

He leads me out into the rose garden.

"You look stunning," he says.

I have wanted a compliment like that my whole life. But today, on my wedding day, I've never cared less how I look.

CHAPTER 17

Avis

"ANSWER ME HONESTLY, IF YOU saw me near your house with a disguise on, would you know who I was?"

Melonius and I drive in silence.

I nod. I would. Of course I would. Since we are speaking honestly now, should I ask him about me? I don't mean it in a philosophical sense, I mean it quite literally. I decide to do the unthinkable and ask the man a question. "How do you know who I am?"

"I don't live in the Stone Age, Avis Baron. I live in East America. There are cameras everywhere. Wave!"

In stories I've read and heard, the heroine fights hard from the beginning. I've always secretly wondered if maybe, just every once in a while, charm could get you out of a bad situation. I've always believed that if I was captured, it might pay to try and make friends with my captor, at first. Problem is, I have very little charm.

"Is this about my mother?"

"Avis, I don't want to upset you before your sister's big day."

"I don't upset easily." I badly want to ask him about my sister.

"It is not about your mother," he discloses. ". Francesca is not your mother. You don't have one."

"Please explain yourself."

Melonius revels in my desire for an answer.

"You were grown in a lab," he continues after a lengthy silence. "By the group you call the Scepter. You're a virgin birth. You and your sister. The first birth of this kind. Right as the country was dividing. You were both government property. We got Nyx. They got you. We made her a Nancy. You . . . well, you see what they did with you."

I am stunned. "Does everyone know?" Francesca, Thaddaeus . . . Ethan?

"I'm not even sure X knows. It's highly classified."

"I thought he was the God of the East."

"He certainly thinks so."

I consider this for a moment. I expect to be devastated. Instead, I feel . . . I feel . . . like things suddenly make sense. "Whose—"

"I don't know whose DNA they used," Melonius divulges, as if reading my mind. "I assume some dead woman that they deem important. Your father, I don't know either. That's over my clearance."

"Please explain who you are, Melonius."

"I am the vice president of the Eastern States of New America, Avis. Would you believe me if I told you no one has asked me a question about myself in a long time? I like you, you know. You remind me of Francesca when she was young. We went to school together."

"How did you end up here? How do I not know who you are? I've never heard of you."

"X doesn't like the way I look on camera, and he doesn't like people knowing he accepts help. Also—my preference is to move in secret."

"Were you and my mother friends?"

"She was nice to me, because she was gracious. But I had no friends."

I think he thinks this will make me feel sorry for him. It does not.

"Neither did I, not until recently," I reply.

We park in front of the White House. It's crumbled, and pieces of it are falling down. It doesn't look like the picture on the old dollar bill. It looks, unlike everything else in the East, a mess. It's too big to make a façade for, too old to fix. It looks like they've just given up.

"Watch out for the rats."

I don't feel fear. I sense something else. An old, familiar tug. I sense my sister. I feel that she's here, I feel her in my bones. I don't sense her panic, or her fear, or her anger, just her heartbeat. Steady and slow.

We enter a side door and go down a dimly lit highway. He opens a coat closet and pulls on a light. In it hangs a puffy, green and gold brocade gown. It reminds me of a tablecloth.

"Put that on. I'll wait outside."

He does, and I do. We walk outside to a large garden. About a hundred people are already sitting down, waiting for the wedding to start. Mostly men, many Nancys, a few women that look like Nancys but have slightly different hair colors.

"Your first time at a wedding, and my first time with a date," Melonius winks.

Maybe he won't kill me after all.

I sit down in my white wicker chair and look around. It's everything I've seen in propaganda videos. It's beautiful, the people are beautiful, I guess. Well the women are. In their Nancy way. Every woman: hair, skin, eyes. It's all the same. I wonder who their mothers are.

I look around for my sister. I don't see her.

There's no music playing. A party with no music? Though I guess a celebration of one-sided ownership isn't much of a party. *Test tube baby. Virgin birth.* The words pop in my mind.

Melonius sits at my left. At my right is another Nancy.

Virgin birth. Sister. East America.

I need an immediate distraction. I introduce myself.
"Hi, I'm Avis."

"Hi, I'm Nancy."

"Uh . . . what number?"

"I'm the first one. Nancy1."

"You're a prototype, huh?" I am too, I realize.

She nods. She either knows exactly who I am, or isn't supposed to ask questions.

Then, he enters. President X. To deafening applause. He is far uglier in person than he is on television, a man made by hand—bad plastic surgery and fillers. If we are made of dust, and to dust we shall return, what do these people return to?

He stands at the podium, a blobfish dressed in a purple gown that reminds me of the old-fashioned priests I've seen in history books. His hair is lustrous, but moves in a very unnatural way. He is easy to hate, regardless of who he is. His whole being radiates with pomposity. My poor sister.

Nancy1 claps so hard I expect blood to burst from her palms; X takes in the applause for ages, and then addresses the crowd.

"We are gathered here today to bring me, your Lord and Leader President X, in coverture with this lovely young specimen, Nancy159. Before the ceremony begins, I'd like to speak a little bit about the importance of marriage for East Americans. Women in the East have the luxury of not having to fight tooth and nail to form something all men are required to form: an identity. A legacy. They are fortunate in that they must only hope that someone finds them worthy enough to join them to him."

There is a murmur of agreement in the crowd.

"And as Eve came out of Adam's rib, Nancy159 will enter my fold. She will have no worries. She will have no more to plan, she will be free to live out her days in pleasure and servitude. No choices. No identity. She will be truly happy. Nancy159 is worthy of this gift, and I give it to her with love. I hope you will give your wives, future wives, and daughters the same, if they are also worthy."

The crowd cheers as one.

I look at Melonius. He cheers too. Covertly, I loosen the straps on my heels. I want to be able to run at a moment's notice.

"And now, the ceremony will begin. Please refrain from photography. The bright lights confuse my poor wives! Oh, and while we usually have the mother sit in the front row and the father walk the bride down the aisle, we were unable to procure those citizens. Never fear! We have an . . . aunt here for her support, and my right-hand, Melonius, will escort my beautiful young bride."

X's voice is orange, the worst kind of orange. Almost mustard.

An aunt? I look around. I can't see beyond a few rows in front of me. I look to my left. Melonius is gone. I look to my right and Nancy1 smiles at me blankly. Can I rescue her from this? Do I need to be rescued? I take my heels all the way off and put my feet in the grass. My heart pounds and then a beating drum starts. Maybe it's a beating heart? It's outside me and inside me and everywhere. The crowd *oohs* and *ahhs*, telling me this is new for them.

I look at X. He is smiling, but something is off. He looks . . . worried.

A door from the White House swings open and a Nancy comes out. She is dressed as a bridesmaid, I suppose. She is probably thirty . . . but it is hard to judge. She walks down the aisle with a basket. She litters fake flower petals on the ground.

"A learned woman makes a man's dark predilections come to light," she sings in a monotone, over the beating heart. The crowd echoes a refrain.

I do not. Nancy1 looks at me with confusion.

The bridesmaid joins X on the stage, kisses him, and stands to his right. A second Nancy arrives. She looks more vacant in the eyes than the ones who surround me. "Nature intended women to be held in joyous slavery," she sings.

A third Nancy comes out. Three wives for one troll of a man. She carries an incense burner; the smell of lavender wafts over the procession. Combined with the sound of the heartbeats, it is all extraordinary in its beauty and strangeness. I look closer and notice the layer of plastic over their gauzy dresses. "Marriage and family are women's only gifts," she sings.

These sayings, they are so awful. You think they'd at least rhyme.

I don't want to attract too much attention, so I mouth the refrain.

A fourth one. She holds a ribbon on a stick. She does not speak at all. She dances beautifully with the ribbon.

Nancy1 leans over to me. "She's mute. It's a beautiful gift."

At the end, when she kisses the hobgoblin, everyone claps. She is clearly the favorite. He probably likes that she doesn't talk. These poor women are reduced to their bodies. I try to put myself in their shoes, try to imagine how I could think this was okay if I was born into it. *Brains* are the treasures of the women of the West. I never questioned that. Perhaps they never question this, either.

A fifth one comes out. I gasp . . . she cannot be more than fifteen. She is tiny and looks prepubescent. She twirls her dress and opens her mouth. She closes it again. She opens it. Words come out as if they are against her will. A beautiful song in a strong, pink voice.

The moon ties the earth to my body.
The sky ties the heart to my sun.
And even if you have my soul
Its song cannot be won.

All the Nancys sing along. The crowd murmurs. I hear concerned whispers. President X looks alarmed, but then he laughs it off.

"I like when they sing," he says, a fake Southern twang in his voice. He's added it since the beginning to sound "folksy," but often drops it without thinking.

"How did you know that song?" I ask Nancy1.

"I don't." She smiles at me blankly.

"I like it," I tell her. I recognize it from the video of the pageant. I recognize it from . . . somewhere else.

Her eyes glimmer at me with an expression that looks like rage. I look for anger inside myself, but I only find pity.

Everyone rises. The heartbeat grows louder. This is it.

Melonius and my sister appear on the edge of the aisle. Her face is blank. She stares straight ahead, showing no feeling, no acknowledgment of the crowd. She wears a long, lace dress as well, no plastic outside of this one. She is completely covered. Turtleneck, sleeves, all white lace. Not even the pound of makeup she's wearing can mask the dark circles under her eyes. I look at her and I see myself. How could they have done this to us?

Melonius starts to walk forward, holding my sister's arm. She does not budge. As if they planned for things to go wrong, a smiling, suited gentleman walks up and grabs her other arm, and the two men carry her, slowly, down the aisle, so it appears almost as if she is walking.

She passes me, and I realize I am crying. Sobbing.

"Your emotion is beautiful," Nancy1 says to me. My first instinct is to hit her, but then she takes my hand. The things she must know. The things she must not know. She is blameless in all this.

As my sister passes me, her eyes move in my direction. Liquid drips down her legs and stains her dress. She has urinated on herself. My sobs grow louder.

She plants her feet. She turns around. She looks at me. A flash of recognition crosses her eyes. And the heartbeat grows stronger. I can *feel* it in my bones. In my blood. My own heart begins to beat in time with it. I think: my sister controls my heart. Maybe she always has.

I never dreamed fear could feel this real. When I watched horror films from Old America I would scoff at the characters as they cowered, laugh at them as they prayed to their gods. But now, I can't think of anything to do but pray. *My Goddess. Please don't make her do this. Stop this. I know I don't know you, but you must be just. Please, for all that is good, stop this.*

They carry her a few more feet. She drags her feet now, obstinate.

"No!" I shout. "No!"

No one hears me over the heartbeats. Or maybe everyone does and no one cares.

As she passes the front row, I see women stand. They contrast with the Nancys: they look like individuals, they wear black dresses. I walk to the edge of my row to get a better look at them. It's Francesca! She's the aunt they spoke of? It's my mother. *Our* mother. They brought my mother here. She sobs harder than me. I don't care where my cells came from, Francesca raised me to be who I am, and I am so grateful to see her now. Rage boils up, bright and harsh over my sadness. The Scepter surrounds her. The Scepter is here. There is no way they came here for this. They must have thought they were coming for "peace talks," only to be humiliated. Mears spots me; she taps my mother. My mother looks at me, fear crosses her eyes, then anger, then understanding. She puts one finger over her mouth, as if to warn me to keep quiet.

Nyx joins X at the podium. Altar. It's an altar. We don't have religious ceremonies in the West, but I know what it is. I know what it means. It means someone, something, will be sacrificed. I have studied the old religions. I am certain this charade is not what they intended.

The monster puts a hand around her waist to steady her. "It is today with great pleasure, that I offer you all as witness to this beautiful sacrament," he says.

Nyx looks out over the crowd.

"Do I, President X, take you, Nancy159, to be my wife for as long as I see fit?"

He speaks directly into the microphone, answering his own question.

"I do."

"Do you, 159, promise to be obedient to me until I no longer have use for you?"

Nyx stares over the audience. She mumbles something.

"Speak up, dear," says Melonius. He has backed up from his spot at the front and stands next to me, watchful. His eyes have lost the joy I saw earlier.

The other wives look worried; even more. They look scared. Terrified. The air changes, it feels as if something ominous is about to occur.

"My name is Nyx," says my sister.

The heartbeat gets louder, much louder. The crowd looks around; Nancy1 drops my hand. Her eyes roll back in her head. I put a hand behind her back, concerned she might pass out.

"Nancy1—what does this mean?"

"It means we are all going to die," she replies without pause, and slumps in her chair.

Then, it happens. People begin to wail. They babble in languages I don't understand. A Nancy passes out and falls straight to the floor. The bridesmaids cover their ears. Except for the mute one—she moves quickly to my sister's side. I watch as she stares at my sister; it seems as if she is pleading with her. She is not like the others. Neither is my sister. I take some pride in this, but it does not override my Weaker Emotions. Fear beats through my body like a kettledrum.

A new, low wail fills the room. I look up, because that's where it seems to be coming from. It is a soft wail. I cover my ears when I realize the noise is *inside my head*. I watch Melonius cover his ears. He looks at me. He hears it, too. X acts like nothing is wrong. The wail gets louder and louder until it is a single woman's scream. Another joins in. Another. I look around, but no one's mouth is open. Then, mine is. *I* am screaming. I think I am. It is so hard to tell where I begin and where everyone else ends. Where I begin, where my sister ends.

X takes her hand; I feel his hand in mine as well. I am repulsed.

"I now pronounce us man and wife! Please enjoy the ceremony."

He picks Nyx up like a baby and carries her back into the White House. The other wives follow. The door closes, and the screaming stops. I drop to my knees. All is silent for what feels like hours, but on my watch, only seconds pass. Then, happy music plays. The sun shines down on all of us, and none of us deserve it, because we watched, and did nothing.

CHAPTER 18

Thaddeus

AFTER AVIS LEFT WITH MELONIUS, there were Nancys everywhere. Thirty-eight of them, total. They came, I believe, from the basement, which was locked earlier.

They've offered us no violence. They simply stand in front of all the doors and windows, watching us. They are surveillance cameras. They are ghosts.

I've been watching them here in the living room, worrying about Avis, worrying about this wedding—and wondering, are the men of the East happy that their women are, essentially, lobotomized? I have been taking Amplexus every day for a week now. I did not know if it would work for a male. But I was born a woman. Or maybe it works on everyone? If so, what might it do for a cis-gendered man living in the East? Would it calm their rage? In old America, after women became the more educated, more moneyed sex, the rage started. It festered, and it wore different clothes: Longing for the past. "Concern" for women. Upholding tradition. But it festered and America divided and then the war began . . . I hear a muffled cry in the bedroom. Ethan's been in the bathroom for an hour. He is terrified of these women. They keep touching his hair.

"Krista?" I call out.

I hear a thud. I run into the bedroom where Krista and Avis slept. Avis's things are still here, smelling her unique fragrance of leaves, and sticks, and all things outdoors. I see Krista near the wall, before she sees me. As I watch, my sister bangs her head against the wall, again. *Thud.*

I rush to her and hug her, and I pull her away from the wall. We sit down on the bottom bunk. She begins to cry.

"What is it?" I whisper. I do not let her go.

"They're in my head. They're trying to get me back. They've done it before. I tried to break once and they got me back. I lost control of my bodily functions for eight days. I needed a respirator."

"It's okay, you're safe here." I desperately hope that this is true.

"You don't understand, Thad. I want to go back. I've failed. I failed my calling. I only have one purpose. To be a Nancy. I failed."

I think on this. "Can you go back?"

"No. I would be killed."

That's the answer I wanted. I am all strategy now. I love my sister, but the Amplexus dulls the fear I would normally feel in this situation.

I hold her tight. I try to quiet her crying, still her trembling. I close my eyes and remember her before all of this happened. When she was eight and she used to dress me up in her clothes. When she was nine and she taught me how to throw a ball. When she was ten and she lay under her bed and listened to music for hours. She was a teenager too early. She was a woman too early. She's still a teenager. She's barely a woman. They took so much from her.

I open my eyes. We're surrounded. Nancys. Eight of them have entered the room. I can see more standing in the hallway.

"Do y'all need something?" I ask, calmly.

They blink at me. A couple more squeeze in the door. They push Ethan in. His eyes are wide, and he is silent. They stare at us. They keep staring.

It feels like an eternity. The lights go off. One of them speaks. "Plans have changed. Follow us," she says. "We will bring you to the basement. There's an exit there."

CHAPTER 19

Avis

I MAKE A BEELINE FOR FRANCESCA and the Scepter.

"Mom . . . " Before I can finish I'm in her arms. She's holding me like she hasn't since I was a baby. "I am furious at you, why are you here?" she says through muffled tears.

"I'm saving my sister! My twin sister! Wait, why are you crying?" I ask.

"I'm human," she retorts. She backs up and looks into my eyes. "Why are you crying?"

"You lied to me," I accuse, hugging her closer. "That was *my sister* married to X!"

"I love you, Avis. I'm sorry I kept so much from you. Can you understand why?"

I look at her. I don't know if I do understand, but I nod anyway.

"Look at me, Avis. We have to get ourselves together. We have to pretend we are having a good time. If we don't, they could keep us here. You're already in so much danger." She looks around. "You came alone? Where's Thad?"

"At the pink house in town, with Ethan and Krista," I tell her. Fear passes through her eyes. "A pink one?" she asks. "Are you sure?" She rubs my face without asking, spit on her thumb. She's fixing my makeup. "You look ridiculous," she says. "And Ethan? A houseboy? You're in East America *and* sexing a houseboy?"

"We're not sexing," I say, embarrassed. She looks relieved, but only for a millisecond.

"Why are you here?" I ask her.

"I accepted their invitation to sit in on some peace talks. I had no idea this circus was about to unfold. X told me he called the wedding off. He said he had picked another bride."

"How are we going to rescue my sister?" I ask.

"The Scepter and I have been planning an assassination attempt for months, Avis. Do you think I would let this happen?"

"You just did!" I exclaim.

"I thought I could talk them out of it . . . " my mother says. "We have weapons. We have political capital. We have things that they need."

"They don't even think you're a person, Mom. You think they're going to negotiate with you?"

"That's not true of all of them. You cannot paint the whole country because X is an empowered moron with Mommy issues."

"So what's the plan?" I ask.

"I'm still figuring it out, Avis. But I'm glad I have you here to help. First, we go underground. Do you have regular shoes?"

"I have some she can wear," Mears says.

They all start talking at once. I can't even keep up.

Helplessness. It's a new emotion. I miss my Amplexus, but it's almost as if I can't remember what it felt like to take it.

CHAPTER 20

Thaddeus

WE'VE SPENT FOUR DAYS UNDERGROUND, by my estimate. I don't know exactly how much time has passed, since tech doesn't work down here. There's no sunlight. The electricity goes out for hours at a time. It's dark and strange, but the Nancys have told us the tunnels below the capital are the safest place for us to be right now.

The blue house did, indeed, have a basement. That basement led to a tunnel. The tunnel is available for all East American residents: it's a complex bomb shelter. Krista's been here before. When she left East America the first time. It's how she got out, apparently. I was able to escape over the border—the wall was never that good of an idea. She seems to like it down here, which I first thought strange, but she then she told me it's the first place she ever felt free.

There are people down here, people with jobs, people with money on the outside. That doesn't mean it's nice: it's not. There are bugs and strange noises . . . but there are medical facilities, testing grounds, that sort of thing. During the day, Krista, Ethan, and I like to go to the Cave, a large cave at the end of the tunnel, where they keep all the women, and, surprisingly, many of the women's small children. We bring them food we get from the blue house. They are afraid to go aboveground. Many of them have never been; they are the only free women in the East. Beneath people's feet, they are free. And somehow, we are freer, too. Free from decisions about what we want to look like or to be. The top inch or so of Krista's hair is black as midnight now. Her skin is darkening underground without her bleaching treatments. Down here, it's Maslow's hierarchy of needs. When your needs are safety and survival, you don't think much about politics. I try not to think about what has happened to Avis. Yet with each day that passes I concentrate on how we will find her—and Nyx—and bring them both home to the West.

So each day we bring the women food and supplies. We play games with the little kids. We pretend we're not afraid. I've seen spiders down here that are too big to kill with a tennis shoe. I may be a man, but spiders . . . I can't. I just can't. Krista killed one and the damn thing screamed. It was "just air whooshing out of its lungs," Ethan said; he insisted that they don't have vocal chords. But what does that kid know? There are cats down here, too. Hairless and slinky. They look like aliens. They eat some of the spiders, and some of the spiders eat them.

I ran out of the Amplexus I stole from Avis. I was taking one every three hours. I've learned a lot from Krista and Ethan about how to cope; Krista tells me if you pretend to be brave, you can trick yourself into it. So I close my eyes, breathe deep, hold my breath at the top and bottom of each inhale and exhale, and pretend I'm a warrior. I face my fears that way. My fears are that we'll die down here. Ethan's bright spirit helps me get through every day; I try to emulate him. But I'm a realist. I worry that we'll never find Avis and Nyx, that they'll end up raped or killed or torn up like genetically superior used cars and sold for parts.

Krista's having closed-eye hallucinations. She's hearing people that aren't there say things. Things in other languages. She tells us what she hears, she repeats the syllables, and they are foreign and strange. I write them down, just in case it's some Nancy shit, but I fear she's just losing it. We all are. Four days in the pitch-black dark will do that to you.

We're in the Cave with the women and children right now. I imagine it looks like a bunker after a war—in fact, I wouldn't be surprised if that's exactly what it is. Everywhere you look there are rags, cots, and crying babies. But somehow they keep their heads up. Women have always impressed me that way. Men struggle with strength, myself included. My favorite new friend is Eva. She's in her forties, and she's been underground so long her eyes are grey and her toes are starting to web. But, she's smart as hell. She catches me drifting into space.

"You know," she says. "The Nancys have it bad, but not as bad as the millions of regular women stuck in the East." Her baby, a skinny little boy, wakes up. She takes him in her arms. She rocks him back to sleep. She whispers to me, "When you get partnered here, it's not your choice." She is barely audible. "Aboveground, you're basically sold. Your parents give your betrothed a gift called a dowry. They agree on the amount beforehand, but in some cases . . . if, at the last minute, his family decides it's not enough money, they burn you. To death. It's called bride burning. Burning women at the stake is an ancient practice, but it's never really left us. There are worse things that happen to women in the East, but I will not tell you tales of them." Eva's coarse black hair hangs over her eyes.

"They tried to give us Amplexus down here, well-meaning people like you sent it from the West. They wanted us to have the physical strength and speed to wage war against the Eastern men. They sent us weapons as well. But the pills . . . it made some of us go mad. My cousin, Ruby . . . People were badly injured, cannibalized. Maybe it was because we didn't have the proper nutrients in our systems to make it work? It was sheer terror. But we had to try, I don't blame the West. We had to try everything we could."

She hands me the baby to hold. I think she expects me to object, as I am a man. But I take him. Holding this woman's baby, it reminds me that I am alive. Reminds me to keep breathing. The baby makes my cold, dead heart beat twice.

The Nancys have filled me in on some of what took place. I know Francesca and Avis are aboveground. I think they are alive—Nyx and Krista say they can feel them. I don't entirely believe in that, but sometimes I think I can feel them, too.

I want to go home. To the West, to the home I knew a few days ago, before any of this. I never fully appreciated how privileged we are in the West. Overwhelming dread fills me. What has happened to Avis? Home might not be a reality for any of us for a long time. If it's ever there again.

CHAPTER 21

NYX

"STOP CRYING, 159," X DEMANDS. The first words he utters to me as husband and wife on our marital bed. I don't stop, because I can't. He likes when I fight, but he does not like this. A guard with a sophisticated weapon sits on a chair in the corner, diverting his eyes.

"Do you need Time Alone?" he asks.

I nod no. I'd much rather get this over with.

"Never mind. I know what you need," he growls in a low voice. I think he's trying to be sexy. Before I realize what's happening, I'm over his knee with my wedding dress over my head. I smell the urine on my dress. I stop crying.

"You're going to count with me," he says.

"One," I say. He spanks me.

"Two," I say. He does it again. "You like this, don't you?"

No. I don't like it. But it takes away from the fear and pain and anguish and despair I feel. Physical pain is a welcome distraction.

"Three," I count. He spanks me. He's not very strong. It doesn't hurt very much. The pain isn't enough to distract me and I start wailing again. I saw my sister. And now I'll never see her again.

"Come on, 159," X says. He sits back on the bed.

There's nothing I can say to this man to make things better for me. It's like I'm a house without an alarm system. Without guards. Without a door. With the windows open. I can try my best, but I'll be robbed.

"You ruined that wedding. It was supposed to be my last. Now I'll have to have another," he chides me.

"No!" I cry. The terror of it. "You have enough!"

He hits me hard on the bottom this time. "Who are you to tell me when I have enough? Lay down with me."

In my mind, I can hear 97 in the next room. *Just come to me. Be in here. I'll be in there. Switch your mind with mine, dive deep.* She has already experienced this. I will not make her experience it again. I wouldn't wish this on my worst enemy. I cannot fight. I cannot move. He kisses my face and my forehead. I stay completely still. He rubs me in places no one has rubbed me before. My body reacts, it betrays me.

His heavy weight is on top of me, and I think this is what dying feels like. I slip away from myself. I take the memory 129 gave me of the ocean and put myself in it, while he puts himself in me. I see the sunlight glint on the water. I see my sister's beautiful face. In my mind's eye. She holds my hand. I turn to my left. 97 is there. She holds my other hand. We all look out at the ocean together. He is right. This is what I wanted. This is everything I ever wanted. I just didn't know there was anything else.

"I love you," he whispers.

He doesn't love me. It is just a thing you're supposed to say. He is done in a few minutes, but it feels like forever. I close my eyes and pretend to be asleep. He leaves me and takes part of my spirit with him. All of my childish dreams of living the privileged life of a Nancy were nightmares. Now they're coming true.

CHAPTER 22

Avis

MY EYES OPEN AND I AM in a strange place. I cannot move my eyes very easily, but it appears I am in a clean, bare, white room. No windows. I have spent much of my life underground, due to war, and it feels like I'm underground now. I conclude I am most likely in a bunker. I am in a white plastic chair, and I am tied to it. Ankles, knees, hips, wrists, arms, forehead. All strapped in. The next thing I notice is that I am naked. I am cold and I am naked, strapped in a white plastic chair. I do not have to urinate, which is strange upon waking. I try as hard as I can to look to my left, and it appears there is a catheter there. It could be an IV though. Am I dead?

In the right corner is a hologram tech. On the tech is a small video feed of me. It connects to somewhere outside.

I am being watched. I decide I am most likely drugged. Not with Amplexus, or else I would have broken this chair in half by now. Most likely a heavy dose of benzodiazepines.

There's a knock. I don't see a door.

"Avis?" a female voice says. I don't respond. The door opens. In walks a Nancy, but her eyes are green instead of blue. She wears a lab coat.

"Avis, I'm Nancy. You might feel confused right now. I'd like to remind you to continue to breathe. We're here to help you, not hurt you. Damage has been done to you, and it needs to be reversed."

"Which one?"

"What?" she replies.

"Which Nancy?" I counter.

She laughs. "It doesn't matter." She presses her arm. An image of a Nancy comes up.

"First words that come to mind, please."

I open my mouth to speak.

"Just think them. I can hear you."

How did I get here?

"That's not important. What do you think of us?"

Robots. Pity. Sad.

An electric shock goes through my body. It feels like a dozen needles going into my abdomen.

"That is a starting place, but a false one."

She opens my mouth with her hands. She puts in a piece of paper. It dissolves in my mouth.

Again. I hear in my mind. My mind is blank.

Better. Try again.

The colors swirl, I see light illuminating from the pictured Nancy.

What did you give me? I think to her.

I receive another shock. Drool drips down my chin.

Lights? People? Colors?

She smiles. "That is much better, Avis," she says aloud. So much improvement in one session. I will be right back.

Don't leave, I think.

She leaves, smiling on her way out. She leaves me alone for a long time. The picture of the Nancy changes, from a stoic expression to a smile. I smile back at her. My consciousness suspends. It seems I have been in this room for hours, days, months, years, eternity.

The door doesn't open, but someone appears inside my room. Two of a someone. All see-through, segmented, clicks and elbows and knees and transparent skin and tiny heads. The Moth Twins are here! The Moth Twins are here to save me!

Beneeva. I think as hard as I can. It's been too long. They make a sound, a sound like squeaking violins, and I am sure they are laughing at me. One touches her transparent, thin arm to my mouth. They do not have hands, but it doesn't look like they are missing anything. At the end of their arms, they glow.

"You can speak now," Beneeva sibilates. There's no time for speaking so I don't. They put their faces close to mine, exploring the inside of my mind.

"Why didn't you save your sister?" the shorter one, Tunsia hisses.

Beneeva berates me: "I would have saved my sister, from anything. What is wrong with you? You are supposed to be fearless? Why are you so useless? Ugly and useless and with no purpose? Just because you are born from a test tube with a famous aunt doesn't mean you can ignore your calling."

I don't remember them being so mean. "I tried to be good. I tried my best to—"

"You have a calling now. You can be with your sister. But you have to choose it."

"Are you going to kill me?"

Their laughter sounds like violins. "No, we are going to give you life."

"You can be a Nancy. You can marry X. He would like you as well, you are very fertile, Avis. More so than your sister. This is a surprise and a gift. Bearing a child would be your purpose."

No daughter. No daughters. Please I can't, not a daughter.

"Sons. We'll make sure of it."

A picture of President X comes on the screen.

"Think of a word for him." I cannot think of a word for anything. HANDSOME flashes in light before my eyes. SMART flashes below it. TRUE flashes below that. Those words seem wrong. Other ones start to flow into my brain. I can't . . . I can't reach them. I can only reach an image of my sister soiling her wedding dress.

"She took too many pills," Tunsia confides. "She wanted her day to be perfect and to be relaxed but she overdid it. She has a drug problem. We are healing her."

A drug problem. That is so sad. I don't want my sister to have a drug problem.

"Don't you want to get married? To raise a family?" asks Tunsia.

A word comes from my stomach. It rises to my mouth. Before it does the picture changes to a picture of the person of the word I am trying. *Ethan. Love.*

"Ethan can't fulfill your destiny," says Beneeva. "You can have him, sexually. X approves of that. He can live in a room in the White House. He'll have a job. He'll have an identity. He won't be a slave anymore. You'll both be free. A happy family. And if he gives you a son, you can keep it."

"We will help," Tunsia buzzes.

The lights and colors bounce around them. I didn't know they were so beautiful.

"I love you," I admit to them. They coo and click at me. They put their bug hands on me, their antennae. They feel my heart beating, they look inside my ears, my nose, my everywhere. Beneeva reaches in my mouth and takes out a piece of food that was in my stomach.

"Strawberry!" she hoots.

The picture of President X smiles. FAMILY appears below it. Then LOVE. BEAUTY. TRUTH. Tunsia takes her antenna and reaches it through my eye. I assume she will take it out. Maybe she'll give me a new mind? I was right! She takes them both out. I can see everything. I can see the whole world.

Tick. Tick. Violins. Loss.

I open my eyes. They're still there. The Nancy sits before me.

"They really are something, aren't they?"

The best. I think, or talk, or say, or something.

"I'm going to take you to a place where there is no language. A place right in this room."

I long for this place. I nod slowly. "If I'm not me anymore, who will I be?" I ask the Nancy. "Will I forget?"

"You've seen voices as colors, Avis. Let yourself see only the colors now. You are the color of a Nancy. You have the voice of an angel. President X has the red of power and respect."

As she jams a needle into my skull, she recites lines from memory. "If you were to you no more, but you still could walk through that door, what you would be left for us to see, would there be you? Would there be me?"

Pornography comes on the tech. I've never seen anything like it. I've never seen women submit to men like that. Bile rises in my throat.

I'm shocked again. My body, not my mind. I convulse for what seems like seconds. I try to avert my eyes.

"Keep watching," Nancy whispers.

I do. The chair buzzes at my genitals. It feels soothing.
More words fall out my ears. She recites words to me,
recites them from memory.

> *"I'm nobody! Who are you?*
> *Are you nobody, too?*
> *Then there's a pair of us—don't tell!*
> *They'd banish us—you know!*

> *How dreary to be somebody!*
> *How public, like a frog*
> *To tell one's name the livelong day*
> *To an admiring bog!"*

CHAPTER 23

Thaddeus

WE'VE WAITED FOR SIX DAYS and now we are done waiting. That's . . . I'm bad at math but it's been . . . seventy-two plus—one hundred and forty-four hours. All that time spent seeing and feeling the real horrors of people who should give up but haven't. Sometimes I think we should all just give up. We're losing the fight. Hate is winning. And if the world hasn't turned completely upside down, it is Krista who has devised a plan to find Avis and Nyx.

Krista remembers her way through these tunnels. They are labeled with numbers and letters like streets, and she uses mnemonic devices, just like our mother taught us.

"A goes to 1 because you eat an apple a day.

Right at the yellow 3 is the correct way.

Then you go the gilded way along the darkest P,

and by the time you have to you're at the last one, T!"

That's her rhyme. It makes perfect sense to her. It's a short ditty, but it encompassed about eight miles of walking in pitch-black dark. Now, at last, we are heading down the tunnel that was labeled "T" in blue spray paint. Finally, we get to a door. The door is white.

"Try to open it," she says to Ethan and me. I'm not stupid, so I don't. He is, so he does. He pulls back his hand.

"What was that? It felt like a crab bit me!"

"What is a crab?"

If we ever get out of here, I will take her to see the ocean.

She laughs, and then puts her face down to the doorknob, but instead of looking through the peephole like I think she will, she licks it. She licks it in a way that makes me feel uncomfortable. She keeps licking it until the door opens.

"How . . . ?" Ethan stammers.

"I'm an invited guest. This is the back door. It's for special friends of the president. I told you we dated," she states, casually.

"I don't like this plan," I say. I've had eight miles to think about it and I hate it. I don't want her to do this. "You defected, and . . ."

"X will be happy to see me. Trust me. It wouldn't matter if I blew up the moon."

We walk in the door and into a cold concrete room with a steel spiral staircase and a door at the top. A door that doesn't appear to have a lock at all. A rat scurries by us.

"Okay," Krista says. "So we all know what we're going to do. I'm going to distract him. If I know X, all his wives are right off of the Oval Office, in the big pink room. It's the first door on your left. Wait about ten minutes after I leave, then go in. Just . . . act like you're on business. Get Nyx out of there and I'll meet you back here in the tunnels."

Krista sprints up the spiral staircase and disappears through the door. Ethan and I sit in the concrete room in silence for what feels like forever. Sweat drips down his face.

"Think we're gonna die?" Ethan says.

"No way, they have no idea what they're doing over here," I lie. I can't let the kid have a panic attack. No time for that.

After an excruciating ten minutes pass, we head up the spiral staircase ourselves, wincing each time it creaks under our weight. We pass through the door and find ourselves in a hallway. I see plush carpet, high ceilings; it's a well-disguised rattrap.

The first door on the left has a gold knocker on it. We are men so we don't knock, we walk right in. The room is pink, and exactly as Krista promised, the wives of that bastard X are sitting around, looking listless. No one looks up or acknowledges us. Ethan clears his throat. They notice him. *Really* notice him. He is a handsome kid, and they're married to a gnome, so I am not shocked.

"We need to borrow Nyx—" Ethan says.

"What my assistant means to say," I interrupt, speaking in my most authoritative voice, "is that Nancy159 needs to come with us. Immediately."

One of the women sits up. She gets up on her knees, looking at Ethan like a gopher. "Can he stay with us?"

"No," I say.

"Well then she can't go with you."

"Get someone we have to listen to," another one says.

"I'm a man, you have to listen to me," I growl.

They look me up and down. One comes up to me, circles me like a tiger.

"No, you're not. You're dressed up as a man. You are a woman. What are you doing here? Why do you want 159?"

It's then that Nyx realizes I am here to rescue her.

She says, "He's my fertility doctor. Lay off."

"HE?" one says angrily. "HE? A DOCTOR? What is this, *Alice in Wonderland?* Have I fallen down a rabbit hole? That isn't a man!"

"He's a eunuch," says another.

"He's not eunuch. He's something else," insists the first. She smells me.

"Listen, dearie. I'm the best fertility doctor in the world. Do you want your friend to give you a child or do you want to talk about my junk?"

"Let her go," says one.

Nyx rises to go with me. She nods at me and makes for the door.

"Hold on, please," says what appears to be the oldest wife. "I want to know more about this. Do you dress like a man so women will have sex with you?"

I laugh. "No."

"So you don't want to have sex with us?"

"No, I do not."

"Who do you want to have sex with?"

"That's none of your business."

"I think it's a sex thing," says a younger one. They all agree.

"You're sick. What if someone kidnapped your mom, dressed her up to look different, and then you accidentally had sex with her because you were fooled? That person would be killed. Don't you think people want to kill you?"

"No."

"You're a freak."

I haven't been mean-girled for years. My face is red and my neck is hot. Anger rises in my blood. But it's not really anger, because it's sad, you know? I know that, intellectually, but sometimes being a man means you push your sadness to anger. When a little boy cries, he's told, "Toughen up, son." So he makes an angry face, he growls like a tiny lion. We push everything to anger. Masculinity is a prison, whether you're trans or not. I cannot let my temper get the best of me at this moment. "I thought you Nancys didn't have opinions," I say.

"We don't, but we know right from wrong, and we hate freaks from the West."

I don't say anything. Sometimes silence is the best way to go in these situations. I remind myself that this is a rescue, not a debate. I can't change these women. They're brainwashed.

Nyx takes my hand. "Maybe we're the freaks. We look at him and think he's not even human. How do you think we look to the rest of the world?"

"Beautiful," one says.

"Perfect," another one chimes in.

"We need to go," I tell her as a third looks directly at Ethan and says, "Sexually viable and—"

Nyx interrupts her. "We all have the same names. We look identical. We're all married to the same man. We're not playing a part in an old American movie like you guys pretend." She points to one of the wives. "You're not Marilyn Monroe. She invented her identity. We don't even have one."

They all look at her, shocked. Except one, curled up on the floor. She's crying, I notice.

"Are you okay?" I ask her.

"She doesn't talk," says Nyx.

You're not a freak. You're beautiful. I hear it in my head. *I can see you.* I look at the one that doesn't talk. She does talk. In your mind. She looks at me, eyes big and blue. She really does see me. Bless her heart, I don't like it one bit.

Nyx and I walk slowly into the hallway. The quiet one follows us.

"I'm sorry," I say. "But you can't come with us. It's an appointment for Nyx."

Nyx looks at me and she's so sad that I relent. "Oh, come on," I tell her.

We hurry through the door and back down the spiral staircase. I expect something out of an action movie. Dogs chasing us. Alarms. Men in uniform. But nothing happens. We get back in the tunnel. I thank the Goddess that Krista's there waiting for us. Krista hugs Nyx.

"I'm Thaddeus's sister, and I've heard so much about you," she says.

Nyx gives her a weak hug back.

Krista looks at the mute one. The mute one hugs her like they're long lost sisters. Krista pats her on the back, a bit surprised.

"This is . . . another Nancy. She's another one of X's wives. She's mute," I explain.

"You took *two* of his wives? Thaddeus, that was very unwise." Still, she's smiling.

I shrug. "The ass has four more." Then I ask: "Why are you grinning? You didn't *have sex* with him, did you? With X?"

"Nope. We played cards. I'm the only person in the country that doesn't let him win. He likes a game named Speed. A baby could play it. Where's Ethan?"

"He's right here." I turn to point to him and he isn't behind me. *Shit.* Where is the kid?

We all hear footsteps. Quick ones. From the White House. Ethan opens the door. His hair is a mess and his face is flushed. He carries a small, old, ugly dog.

"Teaspoon!" Nyx squeals. "I thought you were dead!"

"Run! They might be behind us!" he commands us.

"Who?"

"X's security team! They think I stole the Nancys! They're filming! Run!"

We do.

CHAPTER 24

Avis

THE WHITE ROOM IS OVER. Whatever happened in it is over. Now, I have an inside, which is slow and different, but I can feel and hear in it . . . and I have an outside. My outside can't feel or hear too well. Not like Amplexus. Closer to sleep. My heart still beats. My lungs still expand and contract. My eyes still blink. But my mouth won't make words. My legs won't move. I am in a chair with wheels on it. There is a name for this chair. I cannot tell you it because my brain won't make the shape of the word. They took many of my words from me. How did they choose which ones to take?

One good thing: not only voices are colors now. Everything is. It's called . . . it's called . . . I have to tell you later. I can't make the shape of it. But there's a thing, when words are colors, and music is colors. It's not a witch thing, it's a brain wrong-wiring. There is more to it. I cannot explain.

Melonius wheels me into numbers of rooms. Rooms where I eat. Rooms where people look at me. Rooms with doctors. A room with President X in it. He is the president of East America. He looks at me and asks a lot of questions: Will she be able to walk again? Will she be able to talk again? I cannot answer him and no one else can either.

Melonius leaves me there, in the office of X.

X looks close at my face. "Blink once if you can hear me, sweet girl."

I blink once or I'd be lying.

"Would you like to hear a story?"

I blink once. I cannot tell my story, so hearing one would be nice.

"There once was a group of evil witches from all over the world. They are called the Scepter. They wanted to control history. So, behind men's backs, they did. They guided things, and changed things, and the men never knew they did it. They were queens, warriors, wives, all types. One of them, Martha Mitchell, ruined a great man and a great presidency just by picking up the phone. You can't possibly know what Watergate is, it's another story, for another time. Do you understand?"

I blink.

"There were many women like this. Women who they considered heroes. And men with dark skin and genetic predisposition towards violence . . . excuse me, dear, I forget I must simplify things for girls. Big, dark men who hit people and don't speak well. Some of those men did some things that impressed some people. But I was never impressed. Never. Do you know what impresses me? Order. Science. Tradition. Modern medicine. Do you know I've lived for a hundred and fifty years, pet? I am a hundred and fifty-one years old. I know, I don't look a day over sixty-three. I keep it a secret. Don't you dare tell anyone, my darling."

I blink again. I think I'm supposed to.

"I love an agreeable woman, you sweet angel. So Francesca and her friends, the Scepter—they worked with the government and they picked some DNA from those people. Old, dead people. People who live in books. They picked that DNA and they mixed it together and they put it in a tube and the cells joined and they made a baby. They put the baby in a woman, and the baby split in two. When I found out, I said I wanted one of you or you'd both be killed. I got Nyx. I got your sister. Avis means 'desired.' Nyx means 'the goddess of the night.' I didn't know that at the time, or I would have picked you, because your sister turned out to be . . ."

I don't like this part of the story. But he keeps going.

"The problem with them making you like that, my darling, is that you don't have a soul. You're only a jumble of cells, like a plant. So I'm going to make you a Nancy. I'm going to give you a soul. You'll share one with all of them. So you can live in the Kingdom of Heaven, right here, with me. Isn't that great? Oh sweetheart, can you hear me? Your eyes are tired. Can you blink for me? Isn't that great?"

I blink.

He takes the back of my chair and wheels me playfully around the room. We go down the hall and to the right and then I am in a pink room with the wives. Some of his wives. The blonde things. Not my sister. The other ones.

"Girls," he starts. "This is Avis. 159's sister. She is going to be joining us. 159 and 97 are no more. They are dead to us. We will never speak of them again after this conversation."

"But . . . she is brown," one says.

"We'll take care of that. We need to hurry. We're going to need to go to another property, her mother and the Scepter's attempts have been thwarted, but they will not stay away for long. I'm going to marry her first; I want to marry her like this. Marry her brown like she is. Maybe I'll make a different type of Nancy. A slanty-eyed, brown one. Like the old Orient."

"What number is she?"

"Oh, let's not make her a number! Let's give her a letter. This new prototype, she's NancyA. She's adjusting right now to some treatments so I am going to leave her here with you ladies, but please don't touch her feeding tube, it can come undone. I'll be back before the wedding. Help her get dressed, please. Put a wig on her. Shave her head first if you have to, it's going to be hard to fit anything over that kinky hair. She can't talk, but she blinks. Once for yes, twice for no."

He leaves, whistling. The women look at each other. They do not talk.

"Can you hear me?" one says. "Avis?"

I blink.

"Her name's not Avis anymore."

"You don't become a Nancy in one day. This girl . . . they did something to her."

"It's probably what they did to us."

"In a day? Our transformation took years. 3's took ten. 159 only did three years and she went bat shit crazy. She crawled down a pipe and lives in the sewer now."

"This girl isn't a Nancy. She's barely even alive. He might as well marry a cactus. What, is he gonna have sex with her? She can't even move?"

"He likes when I don't move."

"Don't be perverse."

"He does."

"Really? He likes when I hit him in the face."

"He likes when I call him Uncle Stuart."

"Ladies!" the oldest one bleats. "Your manners! Whatever our Beloved decides is correct."

I cannot tell you who says what, it is too confusing. I can only tell you what they say, and that I say nothing.

"I don't know. This feels wrong to me. And 97 is gone? 97 was his favorite! Where is she? In the sewer, too?"

"I don't feel safe. I don't feel safe. I used to feel safe."

I blink furiously. It feels furious. I don't know how it looks.

"What's wrong with her?"

"It doesn't matter," the oldest one says. "You do her makeup. You get a wig. Help me get her out of this . . . whatever she's wearing."

"It's a hospital gown," one whispers.

"I dreamed of this my whole life. She didn't dream of this. She's not a Nancy."

"Why would you question him?"

They are gentle with me. I like their touch. I close my eyes.

"Is she dead?"

"Avis, are you okay?"

I open my eyes.

"Her name is NancyA."

"She is not a Nancy!"

"Because this is crazy! It was crazy for him to marry the last one! And now this one, her twin? A Westerner? 159 was far too young. What is he going to marry next, toddlers? Embryos? A watermelon? We are for the traditional definition of marriage. We fought for this. The man as the provider! The man as the bee! The man as the shepherd! Women as the handmaidens! Women as the flowers! Women as the sheep! A family like family should be. Why this? Why now?"

"Do you think she can reach the Hive?"

"We can try."

They gather around me. Hold my hands. I have felt a feeling like this before. The word for it, I can make the shape of it, it is a blue word, a night word, and it is initiation, I think.

They stay still. They look deep into my eyes. They all have a hand on me. They begin to shake around me. They make noises I cannot explain to you, but they are brown and black and red.

"She's completely transparent."

"What have they done to her?"

Tears stream down the faces of these women. I do not feel what they feel. I do not feel sadness. I do not feel fear. I don't feel anything. I am like a flower. A sheep. A thing. An empty thing. A thing you can forget about, like an old bag in a closet. It would be easy to forget myself. I am tired, so I close my eyes, and I do.

CHAPTER 25

NYX

THADDEUS LEADS ME THROUGH an underground maze of tunnels, stopping to talk to several unwashed women along the way. There's dust everywhere, and things I'm not used to seeing. Bandages. Children. I am tired, hungry, in shock, and for the first time in my life I am free.

The ceiling is uneven. It seems like it was built cheaply and in a hurry, or just a very long time ago, the path of some underground worm monster crawling through the earth, that got tiled over through the years. The floor keeps changing: concrete, tiles, hard-packed dirt. It's a place with more than one story, and I don't know if many of them are happy ones. But mine is.

Thaddeus, Ethan, Krista, 97, and I have been underground for around thirty-six hours. I keep asking how long. I've found a father in Thad, a friend in Ethan, and a mentor and kindred spirit in dear Krista. I did not know people could be this good. Even Teaspoon loves it down here. Lots of people to pet him and cats to chase. The poor cats.

We arrive at the Cave and sit among the women and eat some sort of porridge, I'm told it is called. It's terrible but it's mine and no one can have it but me. These are my moments and no one can have them. These ideas are so new to me, it feels like tentacles are growing out of my back, grabbing onto everything around me. Krista calls it "Waking."

I'm finishing my glop when I hear the clomping of boots coming down the corridor toward the Cave. They've found me. I hide under one of the bunk beds and close my eyes. I cannot go back. I won't go back. I would rather die. I hear voices all around me, but they don't sound scared. I open one eye. I look out from under the bunk. The boots are on delicate feet. Small feet under a long, cotton black skirt. They are only a few feet away from me.

I peep my head out. "Hi, I'm Nancy—I mean Nyx," I correct myself. "I'm Nyx. I'm hiding under here and I don't want to scare you."

The woman looking down at me laughs. She laughs and laughs and reaches down and pulls me out from under the bunk. She embraces me. "I don't know if you remember me. I was at your wedding. They called me your aunt."

I don't remember her from my wedding. There are holes in my memories from that day. I remember her voice though, from somewhere else.

"Come with me," she says. Her hair is brown, her skin is soft, and she has the grace and beauty of a Goddess. "I will tell you who you are."

Applause fills the area. I look around, and I see that there are other women dressed like her. Middle-aged women, of all shapes and sizes. They talk to Thad, Ethan, and Krista.

"These are my friends. They are the Scepter," says the first woman, and then she introduces herself as Francesca. We sit down on an empty bunk. She tells me what I already know. And then some more. My origin story. I guess we all have one. Thaddeus told me his. Krista told me hers. Mine started in a lab, and then moved into Francesca's uterus. She carried me and my twin, my sister Avis, for nine months.

"Your genes. Your spiritual and genetic mother and father. We had so many ideas. Mary Queen of Scots, Martin Luther King."

"Beyoncé," Thad adds. I don't understand that reference.

"For your father, we wanted an ancient DNA, something really special. We used the DNA of what we believe to be one of the original *Homo sapiens*. The religious call him Adam. He was black as midnight, and he lived a very long time ago. For your genetic and spiritual mother, we wanted a survivor and a revolutionary, but also an ancient.

We chose Kittur Chennamma, a leader in a country called India a very long time ago. She led a movement toward independence, and we wanted the same for you and Avis. They are not the most famous people on earth, or the most famous people in history. We did not pick a great beauty or a great entertainer: we picked trailblazers. Because in this world we needed you to do two things: forge paths, and endure. So that is who you are. Just by surviving, you have honored your heritage more than you know."

The women have gathered around my bunk. "May you carry her light and her genes," they chant. They don't chant like Nancys do. It's different: their minds are separate. What a wonderful moment. I enjoy every second of it.

"He has Avis," Francesca tells us.

Who has Avis? I think. I forget sometimes. "Who has Avis?" I say.

"X," Francesca admits.

"No! Not Avis! Not her too! Not us both!"

They watch me in horror for a few seconds, silent. "Stop it!" Krista demands. "You're going to pull your hair out."

I didn't even know I was pulling on my hair.

"Why did you save me? Someone should have saved *her!*" I look at the faces around me and find only compassion. "He is going to want her as his bride. He will do things to her mind, he will bend her to his will. He will marry her, then he will rape her."

"We will save her. We have tried. We will try again," Francesca whispers.

"They have biological weapons," a woman hisses.

Silence.

"Did he rape you?" Ethan asks, as if he cannot imagine it.

I do not answer, because I do not need to. Everyone hugs me at once. Tears wash out of me in buckets. I didn't realize my body was so heavy.

"He can't get you here," says a woman in the Scepter. She has short hair and kind eyes.

"So what now?" Thaddeus asks. "Tell me what to do."

"I have a friend . . . an old colleague . . . on the inside. I think he will help us. I hope he will come through," Francesca says.

"What if he doesn't come through?" I demand.

"Then we wage war," Francesca says. "We have weapons—chemical and other kinds. We will kill them. We will kill them all."

"No," I tell her. "No. That is how they do it. We will wage war as women. We will wage war as *humans*." I wipe the snot from my nose and I get up on the bunk.

"What are we going to do, try to enact policy? That's not going to work," another lady says. I ignore her. I have something to say. I will interrupt if I have to. Now is different than before.

"Ladies and . . . other folks," I announce. "We're going to stop this. We're going to change things. Pack your things. Because tomorrow, we're not going to live in the dark anymore. I am the daughter of the beginning of earth, the daughter of India, I am a Nancy and your friend, and I am going to lead you to the light."

They roar.

"We have to capture him. All we have to do is capture him. The Nancys . . . I can use them. Can you help me do that?" I ask the Scepter, my friends, my army.

"I have a new Amplexus complex," Francesca says. "It makes you who you really are. In your heart. It strips away your façades and you're unable to be anything but yourself. It robs you of the ability to lie to yourself and others about who you are or what you want."

"That won't work for X. He's a monster," Thad says.

"No. He's not. That will work. I know him. I know his spirit," I say.

"He raped you," Ethan says, still shocked.

I climb down from the bunk and face them all. "Rape is about control. He feels a lack of control. He also felt an entitlement. That is learned. I do not forgive him. But I believe everyone is good at first, everyone's authentic self is good, until they are covered in fear. Maybe there are exceptions, but X is not one. We can't save him, but we can capture him, if he's reduced to his true self," I tell them.

The Scepter erupts with dissent.

"She's just a baby!"

"She's still a Nancy!"

Francesca quiets them by lifting her hand in the air. I love her in that moment.

"We will listen to Nyx," Francesca says.
"Get packing!" Thaddeus yells.
And we do.

CHAPTER 26

NancyA

SINCE YOU LAST HEARD FROM ME, one thing has changed. I remembered one thing. I can stand. I can move one foot in front of another, and I can speak. The wives helped me remember these things. They put them into my brain. They said I cannot get married in a wheelchair, drooling on myself.

I still drool on myself, so they did not win.

I can't tell you a story of my feelings about my wedding day. My brain can't make the shape to tell you about my emotions. I can only tell you the facts. It was much quicker than Nyx's wedding. It went fast. No bridesmaids. No procession. Just people sitting in an audience. No songs, or applause, or fanfare. I did not see anyone smile. Instead of vows, we shared a cup of wine. They said words about things. They gave sermons and talked of marriages past. They did a lot of things I didn't understand and I can't tell you what they were. My brain can't make the shapes anymore. I stood in front of the people. I remember standing now, so I can stand anywhere, which I could not do yesterday.

It is time for more wine now. Melonius hands the wine to me. He kisses my cheek.

"Do not drink this," he whispers.

I did not drink the wine.

President X watches me.

"Why didn't you drink?"

I don't feel like I should tell him. He hands me back the cup.

I drink of it. He drinks of it, too. It's then that I forgot standing again. The altar is about hip height, a grey slab of marble, so I lay on it. I put an arm on each side, and turn my head to the audience. Words form back in my mind. Just a few. The audience looks interested. I realize they think, because I am prone, it will be some sort of sex thing.

It's not a sex thing.

X gulps down the whole cup. Then he takes the decanter, pours another one and drinks it, too. They definitely think it's going to be a sex thing. They don't know I don't remember standing. Or a white room. Or my sister. I don't remember those things. I push them in the back of my mind. I can make the shape of the words but there are no pictures that go with them.

A song in Arabic starts. One I have heard before. Down the aisle, a proper procession comes in. Poor women in rags, hundreds of them. I smile. I love these women. I can see the strength in their eyes. They squint in the sun, as if they haven't seen it in months. Then, someone else enters. My mind makes the shape. He is the color of plum.

He is Thaddeus.

Francesca follows.

Krista.

Ethan, my love Ethan.

Nyx.

They see me on an altar. They think this is going to be a sex thing, as well.

Nyx raises her hands to the heavens. All the Nancys rise.

"Oh shit," cries a man in the audience. He runs out of the rose garden, jumping over a plastic rosebush. A few men follow him. I feel like they know what's about to go down. I feel hope, bright yellow, but I don't let my mind make the shapes, I cannot handle any more disappointment, any more pain.

Everyone's eyes turn to President X, my husband now, I guess, because we drank some wine together. Something is wrong with him. The drink affected him, somehow. He is sniveling. Crying. Carrying on.

"Mommy," he cries. "Mommy! I'm hungry. Mommy!"

I can't feel pity for him. I don't think anyone can. Maybe we should, maybe we should be able to pity this man who's been drugged to be reduced to a child.

Nyx walks up to him. "Motherfucker," she carols, a singsong greeting. He is down on his hands and knees, crawling through the aisle. She follows him.

"Do you like that now? Do you like when I sing that now?"

"Just let me die," he begs.

"You don't get to die," Nyx hisses. I smile. My heartbeat is loud in my chest. But it's not just mine. It's all of ours. The heartbeats have returned, just like at Nyx's wedding. It's not just the Nancys now. It's all of us.

The Nancys begin to laugh. He stops crying. Rage builds inside him. "How dare you laugh at me! Don't laugh at me! Stop laughing!"

They don't stop. X runs into the White House.

"Follow him," Nyx says. Fifteen women in rags and three members of the Scepter follow him inside. They do not chase him. They walk slowly, deliberately after him. They don't look scared. It's not Amplexus that's driving them forward. It's just bravery, plain and simple.

Can you see all these shapes I'm remembering? All these words coming back to me? I sit up on the altar. People cheer for me. For sitting. Not sure I deserve it, people sit every day. But people do heroic things every day, and no one even notices. No one even knows.

"This is the best wedding I've ever been to," Melonius says.

"I knew you were my friend," I tell him.

"I always was, Avis. Your mother. I love her."

I smile at him. He bows to me. I put my hand on the top of his head, like a blessing. I'm no one to administer blessings, but it is my wedding day.

Inside the White House, I hear screams. I walk toward the house, Nyx takes my hand and we walk together. The things that have happened in there. I cannot walk very fast. It's okay, there is no rush anymore. The women file out of the house as we walk in. They go every different way, to all ends of the earth. President X's body hangs from the ceiling. He is dead. Whatever happened, it happened quickly. I will never know who killed him, we will always assume it was all of us. With the help of our allies. He will never touch us again.

CHAPTER 27

Thaddeus

WE'VE BEEN IN THE EAST for four months. The Scepter are busy taking over the country. Freeing women, curing disease. They do their best. I work with the underground women three days a week. But today I'm in the Nice Room for Mean Things, drinking with the Nancy-No-Mores. Teaspoon is sitting in my lap. We drink "mimosas," but there's no orange juice. We simply mixed terrible champagne with ancient pink lemonade powder we found in the basement. The Nancy-No-Mores, his old wives . . . they have names now, they picked them themselves. The mute one, 97, she named herself Atticus. She wrote it on a piece of paper.

Nyx enters. I hug her; she flinches. She still flinches when she's touched. She's asked us all to keep trying, and if she doesn't want a hug, she'll just say no. She often does. It's nice to be taking care of her. Avis comes into the room with Ethan.

"We made waffles!" she announces.

"*She* made waffles," Ethan corrects her.

They are burnt yet still, somehow, frozen. We all laugh and it feels so good.

Avis is also learning how to play the banjo. Francesca has agreed she can date Ethan when she's eighteen, but I know they're sneaking around together.

Francesca took the new Amplexus and stopped taking the old one. Everyone did. Women are rebuilding themselves with love. Women and men aren't that inherently different; I have a unique vantage point, being trans, and I can tell you a lot of their differences are learned. One of the biggest differences, though, is that women aren't taught to go straight to anger, so their access to love is quicker. When the East is won, when the countries are reunited, boys won't be told not to cry. And little girls won't have to deal with their anger by taking a pill. So much could go wrong. So much is still wrong. Everything isn't perfect—but Avis and Nyx sitting next to each other, looking more like themselves—more like each other—everyday? That's a start.

ABOUT THE AUTHORS

Christina Cigala is a writer and producer residing in the wilds of Los Angeles. She writes and produces television for MTV, Fox, Syfy, Speed Channel, HGTV, VH1, Spike, and TruTV. As a playwright, her work has been widely produced in regional theaters, New York, and LA. She has an MFA in Playwriting from the Actors Studio Drama School in New York and a BA from Baylor University.

Bobby Goldstein is the president of Bobby Goldstein Productions and the creator of *Cheaters*, one of the longest-running syndicated shows in history, now airing daily in 215 U. S. markets and in over 100 foreign countries. Goldstein has become recognized for his ability to spot cultural trends and capitalize on rebellious ideas.